"I can't k... and my son know. I can't see what you both see. I will never be able to fit into your world."

Jeremy absorbed the pain that came from Abby's admission, even as he felt the shock that he could still be hurt.

"But in some ways your life isn't so different from what I faced," she continued. "I was the prettiest girl in school, the one everyone wanted to date, the one everyone wanted to be seen with."

"Is that your argument for identifying with my life?"

"Maybe not, but my point is that nobody ever really took the time to get to know me. They never bothered to look deeper, to find out if there was something more than a pretty shell. So I can understand how it might have felt for you when they didn't bother to look deeper than how you think. I think there's more to you than a brilliant reclusive outcast."

"You're wrong," he said. "That's exactly what I am."

Dear Reader,

We have some incredibly fun and romantic Silhouette Romance titles for you this July. But as excited as we are about them, we also want to hear from *you!* Drop us a note—or visit www.eHarlequin.com—and tell us which stories you enjoyed the most, and what you'd like to see from us in the future.

We know you love emotion-packed romances, so don't miss Cara Colter's CROWN AND GLORY cross-line series installment, *Her Royal Husband*. Jordan Ashbury had no idea the man who'd fathered her child was a prince—until she reported for duty at his palace! Carla Cassidy spins an enchanting yarn in *More Than Meets the Eye*, the first of our A TALE OF THE SEA, the must-read Silhouette Romance miniseries about four very special siblings.

The temperature's rising not just outdoors, but also in Susan Meier's *Married in the Morning*. If the ring on her finger and the Vegas hotel room were any clue, Gina Martin was now the wife of Gerrick Green! Then jump into Lilian Darcy's tender *Pregnant and Protected,* about a fiery heiress who falls for her bodyguard....

Rounding out the month, Gail Martin crafts a fun, lighthearted tale about two former high school enemies in *Let's Pretend*.... And we're especially delighted to welcome new author Betsy Eliot's *The Brain & the Beauty*, about a young mother who braves a grumpy recluse in his dark tower.

Happy reading—and please keep in touch!

Mary-Theresa Hussey

Mary-Theresa Hussey
Senior Editor

Please address questions and book requests to:
Silhouette Reader Service
U.S.: 3010 Walden Ave., P.O. Box 1325, Buffalo, NY 14269
Canadian: P.O. Box 609, Fort Erie, Ont. L2A 5X3

The Brain & the Beauty

BETSY ELIOT

SILHOUETTE *Romance*®

Published by Silhouette Books

America's Publisher of Contemporary Romance

To Diane Eliot.
You told me you wanted to be the best mother-in-law in the world and you succeeded. I thank you for that and for so much more, but mostly, I thank you for Peter.

 SILHOUETTE BOOKS

ISBN 0-373-19605-9

THE BRAIN & THE BEAUTY

Visit Silhouette at www.eHarlequin.com

Printed in U.S.A.

BETSY ELIOT

As a teenager, Betsy Eliot's theme song was "I Am Woman (Hear Me Roar)." She's roaring still, now as the author of romance novels. Married to her childhood sweetheart, Peter, she has two wonderful children, Peter and Marie, who have believed in her since they were too young to know better.

Betsy has won several writing awards, including Romance Writers of America's prestigious Golden Heart Award. She served as the president of the New England Chapter of RWA and received the Goldrick Service Award for service to the chapter. She has published two books under the name Elizabeth Eliot. She hopes Helen Reddy would be proud.

You may write to Betsy at P.O. Box 1237, Dedham, MA 02027 or visit her Web site at www.betsyeliot.com.

Dear Reader,

Like all romance readers and writers, I believe in happy endings. For me, this book is proof that they really can come true.

The path to get here wasn't without a few challenges—what would a romance novel be without them? But along the way, I have also had some thrilling moments that I will always remember: winning RWA's Golden Heart Contest, finding an amazing agent willing to take a chance on an unpublished writer, sharing each victory and defeat with a sisterhood of fellow writers and knowing I had the support of my family through it all. Finally, getting the news that Silhouette wanted to publish my book. This is something I've dreamed about for a long time.

So, thank you for sharing this moment with me. I hope you enjoy my first Silhouette Romance and that there will be many more to come. You see, I also believe in happy beginnings.

Best wishes,

Betsy Eliot

Chapter One

It sounded as if there was something being buried out behind the house.

Abby Melrose ignored the sound and pushed the doorbell, hearing the low-toned gong echo through the house. She waited for a servant or perhaps a butler named Igor to answer, but when there was no answer, she rang again. Then a third time, even knowing it was rude. Surely in a house this size there must be cooks or housekeepers, or at least a mad scientist or two.

She looked up at the dark stone exterior of the building and repressed a shiver. It wasn't a castle, exactly, although it looked like something out of one of the spooky gothic novels she used to read before Robbie was born. She didn't have time anymore to read about unsuspecting visitors held in spearing towers or innocent girls wandering through twisted halls.

But this wasn't a chilling mystery novel and there was nothing she'd read about Dr. Jeremy Waters to suggest he had secret homicidal tendencies. Although the fact that he'd been certified as a genius at the age of seven was reason enough to make her jittery. After all, nobody had ever accused her of being too smart—as shown by her presence here today.

Dr. Waters hadn't responded to any of her letters or phone calls, hadn't indicated any interest in helping them. She'd driven over five hundred miles without any guarantee that he would even see them. If she could have come up with any better ideas, she'd have eagerly followed them. That was the problem. She was out of answers and nearly out of time.

When she'd stumbled on an old article about the former child prodigy, she knew she'd found someone who could help her. The story had described his ability to read at ten months and perform complex calculations by seven, reporting his talents with the tone of a carnival barker. A photo had shown a dark-haired boy with thick glasses and an oversize bow tie that made his head look too big for his little body.

Later, as little more than a young adult, he'd opened Still Waters, a school for gifted and talented children. From what she'd been able to discover, it had been a great success, but according to a form letter she'd received when she'd tried to contact him, the school had closed several years ago.

It would have been easier for Abby if it was still open, but she wasn't going to let that stop her. She'd come too far and there was too much at stake to give up now.

She turned toward the car she'd left in the overgrown excuse for a driveway. Robbie waited patiently in the back seat, more patiently than any other five-year-old she'd ever seen. She gave him a cheerful shrug and held up her index finger with the signal to wait.

Trying not to feel like one of those silly heroines who

hears a bump in the night and goes to investigate in her sheer white nightgown, she followed the sound around to the side of the house.

Just beyond the shroud of trees that had contributed to the gloomy feel, the land had been cleared and the hot sun of early summer once again beat down on her.

Instead of a gothic novel, the kind of book she'd been imagining shifted. Abby found her pulse racing for another reason entirely.

There was a man, all right, but he wasn't digging the grave of his recently deceased wife. This was more like one of those books where the innocent, sexually frustrated wife of a neglectful husband stumbles upon the sexy gardener and is overcome with instant pangs of lust.

Well, she sighed, she wasn't innocent, at least. She had a son to prove it.

Abby had to remind herself that she'd outgrown fiction the day Robbie was born. But she could look. She supposed there was no harm in just looking.

The man's back was to her as he stabbed a hoe into the ground, loosening the dirt of a large vegetable garden. His hair was black and long, brushing his shoulders as he worked. An ancient pair of cutoff jean shorts rode low on his waist and hugged his behind when he bent. His shoulders were wide, his back solid, with the kind of powerful build that typically came from physical labor rather than pumping iron in a gym. The muscles in his arms bulged in a ragged sleeveless T-shirt as he swung the hoe and slammed it into the ground in a continuous motion. For a moment she was mesmerized by the swell and clench of the muscles, the almost poetic perfection of the male form. Abby had learned not to put much stock in appearance, but she couldn't deny a purely female response.

She cleared her throat and concentrated on the matter at hand. "Excuse me."

He didn't appear to hear her, continuing with the repetitive motion that seemed to take his anger out on the rocky ground. It was a good thing he wasn't a demented recluse, she thought. She wouldn't have had a chance.

She stepped closer. "Excuse me," she tried again. "I'm looking for Dr. Jeremy Waters."

The hoe slammed into the ground with an angry whack and he turned to face her. The way he was glaring at her gave the impression that he'd known she was there all along.

Abby was used to people looking at her. The startling length of her white-blond hair and the green eyes that had been described as emerald so often that she'd come to hate the stone usually brought about an instant softening effect on the opposite sex.

Not on this man. Soft would be the last word she'd use to describe him. His face was a mass of contradictions, long and narrow with a square jaw and grooves instead of cheekbones. His nose looked like it had been broken on occasion and a tiny scar slashed across his chin. She couldn't see the color of his eyes from this distance, but they were dark like his hair and the brows that scowled at her.

Abby had the strangest urge to run and check her own appearance. The old habit of carefully applied powders and paints caught her by surprise. For the last few years she'd done little more than pull her hair into an elastic and apply a gloss to her lips when she remembered. It was a long way for a woman who had once considered her looks her most valuable asset. That had been a lifetime ago, before Robbie had taught her what was really important.

"Who are you?" he demanded finally.

She jolted at the harsh tone, but refused to let him intimidate her. She'd allowed enough of that in the past. "My name is Abigail Melrose. Abby. I'm here to see Dr. Waters. Is he around?"

He continued to glare at her as if the force of his disapproval would chase her away. She'd have been tempted to take the hint if she had anywhere to run. "I've been in contact with him about my son, Robbie. I was hoping I could talk to Dr. Waters about him."

He stared at her for so long, she began to wonder if he understood. Since people had always taken one look at her and assumed the same, she tried not to judge him based on his strong, silent type.

"You've come to the wrong place," he said finally. "You should leave now."

Abby took a deep breath and wondered what it was about her that made people want to tell her what to do. Her ex-husband had made the skill into an art form, always explaining to her in that smarter-than-thou tone that she should leave the thinking to him.

She wasn't about to give up so easily. "Isn't this the Still Waters School?"

"No."

She frowned at his answer until she realized that technically it wasn't a school anymore. "Is Dr. Waters here?" she tried again.

"I'm the only one here."

Just her luck. She'd come all this way and he wasn't even home. "Do you expect him back soon?"

It wasn't a difficult question, but it appeared to give him trouble. Just when she was sure he wasn't going to respond, he answered, "He's not coming back."

"Ever?"

He shrugged. "I suppose if he left he would have to come back sometime."

"I see." That was as clear as mud. "Maybe I could come back later. I want to talk to him about—"

"Talking's not going to do you any good. Go away!"

This wasn't just ill-mannered. This was rude. No wonder this man was working out here all alone, in the middle of nowhere. "I'm only asking for a minute of his time. Don't you think he could give me that much?"

"Time can't be given away."

Abby paused. It was strange but his comment sounded like something Robbie would say. "That's true, I suppose," she responded finally. "Maybe I could borrow some."

His frown deepened. "Are you making fun of me?"

Her mouth dropped. She'd be the last person to criticize. "Of course not. I'm just trying to explain..."

Once again, he interrupted her. "Were you invited?"

"Well, no, but—"

"Then that's not my problem." He turned away as if their conversation had come to an end.

Abby resisted the urge to stamp her foot. "Look, I've come a very long way—"

"Five hundred and sixty-three miles to be exact," Robbie clarified, approaching from around the house. "At an average forty-seven point six miles per hour, it took us seven hours and thirty-eight minutes, including rest stops. It would have been only three hundred and seventy-two miles if we could have flown with the crows."

Her son, Abby thought, as she turned to look at him crossing the yard, saw the world a little differently than most five-year-olds. She felt the swell of pride as well as the ever-present shock that she'd managed to produce such a remarkable child. Physically she knew he resembled her, his blond hair curling around his head like a bobbing halo, his eyes bright with curiosity and intelligence that no jewel could hold. For her, those looks had been what made her special, but for Robbie they were barely a consideration. She often wondered what hiccup in her gene pool had made him her son.

She stepped closer, automatically drawing him to her side and placing a hand on his shoulder. She wasn't even aware of the protective action until she saw the way the man observed her, coldly eyeing them both as if they were the ones who posed a threat.

"Honey, I told you to stay in the car," she admonished gently. She didn't want to expose Robbie to yet another disappointment and she'd already come to the conclusion that this man had no intention of helping them.

"I was bored."

She couldn't claim to be surprised. He'd flown through the collections of puzzles and brainteasers she'd painstakingly gathered for the trip in the first hour. Despite having the mind of a brilliant adult, he was still a little boy.

"Hello," Robbie greeted the man with a maturity that would have made her doubt his youth if she hadn't actually been a participant in his birth.

"Hello."

Thankfully Abby noted the hostility was missing from the man's voice. Without it, the deep, husky rumble sounded a touch more accessible—and somehow vastly more dangerous.

"My name is Robbie Melrose. We've come to see Dr. Jeremy Waters."

"What do you want him for?" the man asked.

Robbie thought about the question for a moment, while meeting the man's gaze. "I'm not completely certain. My mother has chosen to keep her reasoning undisclosed from me.''

So much for secrets, Abby thought. She should have known she shouldn't try to outsmart her son.

"I'm sure, whatever her reasons, she's doing the right thing. My mother always knows what's best.''

Abby's eyes widened at the compliment. But then again, she was his mom. He had no idea how overwhelmed she was. And she intended to keep it that way. She would never allow her son to think he was a burden. She was all he had—heaven help him—and she wouldn't let him down.

"However, I don't think it's a coincidence that we've chosen this area of the Berkshires for our vacation," Robbie continued. "Although it's certainly a beautiful place, I have a feeling that the appeal has more to do with the intelligence quotient of Dr. Waters. He's got an IQ over two hundred, the highest ever recorded. Mine is only in the one-eighty range.''

The man looked at him blankly.

Abby felt the need to defend the claims. "I've got test scores and evaluations. He really is an extraordinary child.''

He frowned, appearing almost angry. "Those numbers mean nothing to me.''

Robbie nodded. "They're subjective, it's true. But at least they give the testers something to do.''

She could have sworn she saw the man's lips twitch into something resembling a smile before his face settled back into a vacant stare. "I'm sorry, I can't help you. But I wish you the best of luck finding whatever you're looking for.''

"Thank you," Robbie answered, missing the obvious brush-off.

Abby didn't miss it, but she chose to consider her decision to retreat a tactical maneuver rather than a defeat. She wasn't finished yet.

She didn't bother with goodbyes as she took her son's hand and turned back toward the car. Once she had settled Robbie in the back seat, she began the next leg of her trip into the town that would be their home for the summer, struggling now to manage the fatigue that seemed to have finally caught up with her. It was almost as if the stranger had had some dangerous power after all, with the ability to somehow sap her of the rest of her energy.

"Are we going back to Pittsburgh, Mom?" Robbie asked tentatively.

Abby took a moment to make sure her voice would be calm when she answered. "I'm not going to give up on our summer plans so easily." Or her own. "There will be another chance to talk to the famous doctor sometime in the future."

Robbie paused, digesting her answer before following with another. "Dr. Waters didn't seem too willing to help us this time."

Abby nodded in agreement. She wasn't surprised that her son had also figured out who they'd been talking to. He often saw things that other people missed.

"Well, if he thinks we're just going to go away then he's not as smart as he thinks he is," she vowed.

Jeremy Waters listened to the car pull away and dropped the hoe on the ground. So that was the annoying Mrs. Melrose. She'd been pestering him with letters for months, describing how unusual her son was, how different, how extraordinary.

He'd heard it all before.

Not once had she mentioned whether or not he liked

baseball or if he collected stamps. It was always the same, as if the child was one big brain with no other traits of importance.

He'd been expecting the pushy Mrs. Melrose to show up eventually, but he had to admit that her physical appearance had caught him completely by surprise. He'd been expecting the academic world's equivalent of a stage mother, not a fairy princess. She'd been younger than he'd anticipated, probably in her mid-twenties assuming she hadn't had a child when she was a baby herself. Her luminous eyes were fringed with dark lashes. And that stunning blond hair of hers, floating like a cloud around her face—he'd had to restrain himself from asking her to turn around so he could see whether it grew all the way down her back. Then, when she'd turned to leave, he couldn't suppress a glimpse that had given him his answer in the affirmative. As always, it was the quest for knowledge that led to his downfall.

And the boy. Looking at him had been like looking in a mirror. Of course there was very little physical resemblance from the odd little minicomputer he'd been as a child, but the eyes had been the same, wide and inquisitive, taking in everything, thirsty for knowledge. His face was alive with intelligence, forever branding him as different from other "normal" little boys. He recognized the defensive angle of his shoulders, as if the boy could somehow protect himself.

Jeremy knew what it was like to be tested and probed, to be put on display. He'd given up being the main attraction in the freak show of life.

He didn't want people around, especially a woman who looked like Abby Melrose. Although he didn't care to admit it, he couldn't deny that she'd induced a physical reaction from him. It was a conditioned response, he knew, programmed into his DNA to help propagate the species. But knowing the biology of his reaction didn't make him feel it any less.

He supposed, in a way, it was fortunate that he would be unable to help her. Not only would it save his sanity, but it would protect both of them.

Because he would never again involve himself with a young person who had so much potential.

There was too much at stake if he failed. Again.

Chapter Two

Two days later, when she returned to Spooky Mansion, as she'd come to think of Dr. Waters's home, it took five long and annoying rings of the doorbell before it was finally answered—although answered was a tame description of the way he threw open the door and sent it crashing against the wall. Abby got the impression she might have interrupted something by the way he was dressed: rubber gloves reaching nearly to his elbows, a multicolor-spattered rubber smock and plastic goggles covering his eyes.

What could he possibly be doing, dressed like that? Conjuring up the cure to cancer, perhaps, or on the brink of some messy scientific breakthrough? Abby didn't ask. First, because he didn't look in the mood for idle chatter and second because she was certain the details would be beyond her comprehension. It was hard enough keeping up with her five-year-old son. She couldn't imagine what went on in the head of a man who, at age ten, had solved one of the mathematic equations previously thought to be unsolvable.

One thing was for certain. If he hoped to give the appearance of a mad scientist, he was succeeding.

"What are you doing here?" he demanded.

A *maaad* scientist.

"I came to talk to you."

Beneath the goggles, his eyebrows lifted comically. She couldn't be sure if he was surprised that she'd dared to return or by the stupidity of her answer.

"You don't take a hint, do you?"

"You mean the hint I got from the gardener?"

"So you figured it out," he sneered. "That doesn't make you a rocket scientist."

He wasn't the first to point out that fact. He was right, of course. She didn't have a fraction of the intelligence he had been born with. "But Robbie might be. A rocket scientist or a brain surgeon or heaven knows what else."

"That's not my problem." He ripped the gloves from his hands and yanked off the goggles.

Abby could only stare as she got a closer look at the man who had been called a human computer. He certainly didn't fit her image of a brainy nerd. His face was creased with ragged lines and planes, his mouth wide and sensual, though it twisted now in a snarl. But it was his eyes that really drew her attention. Standing this near, she could see their color, a soft, gentle brown. They made her want to step closer instead of away, as if they held some secret that was vital for her to understand. Remembering the picture of him as a child with oversize glasses, she concluded that it must be contact lenses that gave him the impression of vulnerability.

Certainly nothing about him fit her image of a supergenius, though even as that thought registered, she realized

how narrow-minded it was. How many people had un-
thinkingly said the same thing about Robbie, as if brain
function was somehow related to hair color and weak vi-
sion?

She supposed it was just some misguided attempt to
explain her unusual physical reaction to him. Her palms
were sweating and her heart was beating a little faster, and
her reaction had nothing to do with the visual daggers Dr.
Waters was throwing at her. Although she wouldn't have
admitted it, her response to Dr. Waters the other day was
the real reason she'd run away rather than confronting him
about his identity. She was sure he'd be amused by her
reaction if he knew, but she had no intention of letting him
in on the secret. She couldn't afford the contempt that was
sure to follow her foolishness. She had to convince this
man to help her.

"Dr. Waters, I have to talk to you about my son, Robbie. As I wrote to you in my letters, he's a certified child
genius. His IQ is off the charts. When he started preschool,
his teachers thought he had a learning disability until they
figured out that he was so far advanced. They gave him a
slew of tests and each one came back with more startling
results than the last."

"Mrs. Melrose…"

Abby didn't give him a chance to continue with the
brush-off she knew was coming. "Toward the end of the
school year, I got called in to a meeting with the principal
of the elementary school Robbie was supposed to attend
next year. I figured they might want to have him skip a
few grades since he's pretty much mastered the alphabet
and counting to ten." She could tell the sarcasm wasn't
lost on him. "Instead he told me that Robbie might be
better off if he looked elsewhere for his education."

She knew she was babbling, but she couldn't stop herself now that the words had begun to flow. "The school said that according to his scores, he might be able to skip elementary or even high school all together if he passed a few tests. Can you imagine him in college? He's not even allowed to go to the store by himself."

She wasn't sure, but she thought she caught a glimpse of sympathy through his gruff exterior.

"They suggested home schooling as an alternative." She laughed harshly at the thought of trying to teach Robbie herself, then paused for breath and to control the tears that threatened. "Although they used all these fancy words to explain their decision, the bottom line is that they don't have any programs challenging enough for him. I haven't told Robbie. He'd be crushed if he knew. He's been looking forward to going to a real school since he could walk."

She barely caught the wince he tried to hide. "There's nothing I can do for him here, either."

"That's not true. Most of the higher level schools I've contacted have policies against taking students as young as Robbie and the lower level ones are worried that he'd be smarter than most of their teachers, not to mention the students. Then I read an article about your school and I knew you'd faced this kind of situation before."

"What did it say?" he snapped, his eyes blazing.

"It was a story about Still Waters and the kind of kids who went there. I think it was written right after you'd opened." He seemed to relax and she wondered at the cause, but didn't pause to consider the reason. She had to make him understand. "Robbie would have fit right in. He is different from other children. He has different needs, a different future ahead of him."

His face hardened before her eyes and she'd been so sure it had already been formed out of granite. "How terrible for you to have to deal with such a burden."

She gasped, horrified that he'd gotten the wrong idea. "It's not a burden." Or if, secretly, it was occasionally almost too much to handle, it was a burden she carried with pride. "I'll do whatever I can to help Robbie. He's such an amazing child. He's brilliant, yes, but he's also got this wonderful sense of adventure and mischief. He's a sensitive kid, worried about the future of everyone on the entire planet, and he asks the most thoughtful questions. Unfortunately I don't have the answers for him."

"What makes you think I do?"

"There are a lot of similarities between you and Robbie. You were both very young when your...gift was discovered." Although she was certain both of them would sometimes consider it a curse. "You both have extremely high IQs." She paused, searching for the right words. "You know what it's like to be different from everybody else."

At her words, he froze and she wondered what she'd said to put that look on his face. Then he smiled with malicious satisfaction as if she'd stepped into a trap. "Let me put this in a way you can understand," he said, speaking slowly. "Go back to Pittsburgh. I can't help you."

Abby bristled at the familiar condescending tone, but strangely it was just the bolster she needed. Just because he was smarter than she was, didn't mean he should underestimate her.

She'd been acting under the assumption that he hadn't known about Robbie, but if he recalled where they came from, he must have read the letters she'd sent him. He undoubtedly knew everything. He'd probably known from the beginning. And she'd been wasting her time giving him background information he'd been aware of all along.

"I'm not going back until I figure out what to do with Robbie in the fall," she told him. "We're staying here in

Wharton for the summer, so you might as well get used to it.''

The brush-off he'd appeared ready to give her halted as he stared at her. She could practically see his mind processing this new information. "You came five hundred miles without a backup plan if I didn't agree to help you?"

"Five hundred and sixty-three miles," she corrected, thinking of Robbie's calculations.

His brows furled as if trying to figure out a particularly perplexing problem.

"We're staying at the Sunshine Lodge."

Those same brows lifted with surprise. "Edith Crawley's place? And you still came back here? You must either be very determined or very stupid."

The well-aimed jab should have been expected but it still hurt. She tried not to let it get to her. What he thought of her was unimportant.

It was true that when she'd mentioned contacting him, Mrs. Crawley had entertained her with a number of horror stories accusing him of everything from brainwashing babies to running a cult. Abby preferred to make her own decisions, but so far, everything her new landlord said seemed a possibility.

"We are not going back. Robbie's going to have to make a change anyway, in the fall," she explained. Even if she hadn't figured out exactly where they'd be going, one thing was for certain—she wasn't going to abandon her son. Wherever they went, they'd be together. "I've got money saved, enough to hold us for a while."

He appeared on the verge of arguing with her before he caught himself. "I don't care what you do. Just as long as you don't do it here. Now go away."

"I'm not leaving until you hear what I have to say."

"I don't care what you have to say," he growled.

For Robbie's sake, she couldn't accept that answer. "But you used to be a teacher. Your school—"

"The school's closed. I don't do that anymore."

If Abby hadn't been standing close enough to keep him from closing the door on her, she'd have missed the flash of pain in his eyes. She'd never found out why he had closed his school, she realized. After meeting him, she figured he'd simply scared his students away with all his growls and grumblings, but now she wondered if there wasn't some deeper reason.

From inside the house, a kitchen timer went off. Dr. Waters began to tug his gloves back on and turned to go. Discussion over.

"Wait! You don't understand..." Without thinking, she grabbed his arm.

Slowly, and with great curiosity, he looked down at her hand, considering it as if deciding whether or not to chew it off. He didn't pull away, however.

"On the contrary, Mrs. Melrose. I believe it is you who does not completely comprehend the situation."

She tipped her chin up, refusing to be intimidated. "You haven't even listened to all the facts before making your decision!" she challenged. "What kind of genius are you?"

To her surprise, he burst out laughing. At first she thought he was laughing at her, but then she realized there was no humor in the sound. "That's the first time my intellect has been questioned since I was old enough to walk."

She swallowed and pulled her gaze away from his powerful smile. It was nearly as bright as his mind. "Well, maybe it's about time."

He didn't respond right away, deliberating with great care. For once, Abby remained quiet. She might not have the intelligence to match this man but she'd always been good at reading people. Her best shot now was to let him decide on his own. Then if he made the wrong decision, she'd figure out some other way to push him. It would be no more difficult than budging your average mountain.

"If I listen to what you have to say," he asked finally, "will you leave me alone?"

"Yes," she lied.

He stepped back, throwing his face into the shadows and making himself appear even more menacing. "Then by all means, please come in."

Abby took a deep breath and told herself it was relief humming through her bloodstream. She couldn't run now, though every ounce of common sense she possessed told her to do just that. She reminded herself that he was just a man. But somehow that made her feel even worse. She pictured her son, trying to understand why the kids his age made fun of him, quietly facing the adjustments that had come after a series of tests, looking to her—to her!—to figure out what happened next.

Abby lifted her chin and stepped through the doorway into the world of a genius. Even with every bit of her own intellect on alert, she didn't have a clue about what to do next.

Jeremy analyzed his decision to allow her even this brief opening into his life. Contemplating it from every facet, he concluded he was simply out of his mind.

Actually that wasn't far from the truth. Whenever he looked at the tenacious Mrs. Melrose, he seemed to lose his renowned ability to reason.

He glanced over his shoulder to see if she was still following or if she'd run screaming from the house. No such luck. She was peering with curiosity into each of the rooms they passed. What did she expect to see? he wondered. Caged animals prepared for scientific experiments? Food in pouches, served on petri dishes?

"Do you live here all alone?" she asked.

"Yes. There's no one around for miles." He leered menacingly but she gave no indication that it had the desired effect.

"It's a big house for one person. Did you design it purposely to scare people away?" she asked bluntly.

Jeremy was caught so unprepared by her candor that he answered with equal honesty. "That's just a side benefit. The house was built by an old Hollywood horror film star. It suited my purpose."

"You mean for your school, Still Waters?"

"The school is not up for discussion." His angry voice echoed through the empty rooms.

Abby's eyes widened and he saw a glimmer of fear that she attempted to hide. Still, she continued to follow him. Jeremy didn't know if it was stubbornness or foolishness that made her do so. Although he couldn't be sure of her reasons, at least he had managed to figure out his own. He concluded that allowing her into his home, his sanctuary, was a form of self-torture. Having her around made him recall how different he still was.

He could see every emotion that passed through her mind and knew that she saw him as some kind of freak. Her biggest fear was that her son would end up like him, alone and bitter, unable to relate to normal people. Like the rest of the outside world, she looked at him and wondered what kind of weird and twisted thoughts went on in his head.

He didn't think she'd want to know.

Because despite what she might think, he was a man, capable of reacting to her extraordinary beauty. He'd noticed the shapely figure beneath the simple peach sundress and the way the color of the material made her skin appear even more flawless. He'd seen the beseeching look in those amazing eyes and imagined her looking at him like that for other, much more personal reasons. Yet, he'd also noticed that she hadn't capitalized on her looks as he might have expected. Though she wanted something from him, she hadn't done anything to play on her appearance for the purposes of getting what she wanted.

His inquisitive mind still had a few other questions. Such as why she was persisting in this hopeless undertaking? Comprehending the motives of his students' parents had always been difficult for him. They wanted him to make their kids normal, or worse, to make them even more extraordinary. Abby seemed to want what was best for her son. He was almost certain of that. But if she had rightly concluded that Jeremy was a deviant specimen, unable to live among those society had deemed normal, why would she want to subject her son to his obvious flaws?

"Where's the boy?" Jeremy asked without turning around. There was no use practicing his social graces. She wouldn't be around long enough for it to matter.

"Robbie went to camp today. Since we'll be sticking around, I thought I'd enroll him in the summer program down by the lake."

He stopped suddenly, almost causing her to plow into him. "That's not a program for gifted children."

"I know, but they have swimming and boating. It will be good for him to spend some time outdoors."

He didn't comment, preferring to process the information in silence.

Naturally she didn't allow the omission. "Why? Is there something wrong with the camp? It had a good rating in the travel book of this area."

He was sure it did. They catered to the wealthy who vacationed in the area and their clients were afforded the best in everything. Several years ago, as part of an enrichment program they'd offered, Jeremy and some of his students had been asked to perform complex mathematic calculations for the group. Perform. It was a good enough word for what they'd been asked to do.

"I spoke to the owner myself. A man named Drew Danforth. He seems very nice. He gave me a huge discount because they happened to have an opening at the last minute."

When not running his camp in the summer, Danforth, the town's golden boy, was a three-sport coach at the local high school and the area's most eligible bachelor. And he'd taken one look at Abby Melrose and discovered a last-minute opening at one of the most exclusive day camps in the area? What a coincidence!

Abby was beginning to look panicked at the thought of leaving her son someplace that wasn't safe.

"There's nothing wrong with the camp," Jeremy acknowledged and she sighed with relief. He didn't bother to explain that there would be a much greater danger from himself if he were to help her. He wasn't going to get involved. No matter how persuasive she tried to be.

They reached the kitchen, where the project he'd been working on before he was interrupted covered the wide expanse of counter. He'd opened the windows, but an odd, pungent odor still hung in the air. At least there was ample room; the kitchen had been designed to allow lavish parties. Jeremy could recall when the school had been open and everyone's responsibilities had included pitching in to prepare the meals. Occasionally the behavior of some of the smartest young people in the world could have been mistaken for frat house antics.

Ruthlessly he banished the image from his mind.

"Sit over there," he commanded, pointing to an empty chair halfway across the room. "This substance is caustic if it touches the skin or is inhaled."

Her eyes widened with alarm and curiosity as she did as he asked. After protecting his own eyes with the oversize goggles and replacing the rubber gloves, he picked up a thermometer hooked on the side of an enamel pot on the stove and checked the temperature of the steaming liquid inside.

Although he didn't look at her, he knew she watched his every move.

As he took a long, plastic spoon and began to stir the mixture, it occurred to him that he should have used a metal spoon so that he could watch her eyes when it disintegrated. Next, he approached a second container on the counter, this one an ordinary pitcher that might have been used to serve lemonade. The poisonous contents of the scalding liquid were also being monitored. In order for a successful mix of the solutions, the timing had to be exact.

"Where's Robbie's father?" Even as he asked the question, Jeremy realized he'd asked it for himself. She hadn't mentioned a husband in her letters and he didn't think the omission was accidental, but whether or not Abby had a man in the picture was irrelevant.

Again the chin tipped up. "We're divorced. He left us when Robbie was little. He couldn't handle..."

Revealing more than she'd intended to, she stopped herself, but not before Jeremy filled in the blanks. The boy's father hadn't been able to deal with the freakish nature of his own son. What a fool.

"Doesn't he have anything to say about Robbie's future?" he asked. He would have preferred trying to reason with someone who didn't stare at him with those remarkable eyes.

"He had opinions about everything, as a matter of fact," she said, "and as luck would have it, they were always right. I'm sure he'd be the first to agree with you that I'm making a mistake, but he hasn't been involved with Robbie since the day he left. I'm all Robbie has. There is nobody else."

As far as he could see, the boy could do worse than having her as a supporter. He was certain that after he disabused her of the notion of gaining his cooperation, she'd soon find a better candidate to help her. Someone who wouldn't end up hurting her son instead of helping him.

"You see, Dr. Waters, that's why I need you."

Jeremy dropped the spoon into the mixture where it hissed and sizzled. "Stop calling me Dr. Waters," he snapped. "You make me sound like I'm about to operate on you without anesthesia." Even as he said the words, he wondered why he had removed that barrier. He should be building up walls, not tearing them down.

"The thought occurred to me," she responded dryly.

Jeremy's lips twitched, and he turned his back on her. "All right. You're here. Now tell me what you want so you can leave."

"Well, at least you're keeping an open mind," she mumbled. Taking a deep breath, she continued, "You've met Robbie. He's an exceptional child."

He brought the pitcher to the stove and poured the contents into the enamel pot. The mixture gurgled satisfactorily. "So what's the problem, Mrs. Melrose?"

"Abby. You can call me Abby if I'm going to call you…Jeremy?"

Though she attempted a smile, his name sounded awkward on her lips, as if he shouldn't have such a normal name. He shrugged. It wasn't going to matter what they called each other.

"If Robbie is such a great kid, what's wrong?" he prompted, knowing the answer.

This time, rather than describing her son according to his test scores, she began to give accounts of Robbie's childhood. She described the problems he had with other kids, making friends, fitting in. Jeremy rubbed absently at the scar on his chin, the result of a very juvenile disagreement about the gravity of the moon. He knew how the little guy felt. It wasn't easy being different.

"Because he's so smart," she explained, "he tends to want to be around adults, but he doesn't fit in with them, either."

Jeremy could have told her that age didn't help the misfit phenomenon, but he didn't think it was what she wanted to hear.

As she continued to describe the problems Robbie had faced in his young life, Jeremy's anger grew. Yes, there were issues that other children didn't face but there could be joys, too, in seeing things other people missed, in finding the solutions to complex problems. Like most people, all she saw were the differences.

There was no doubt that her son was remarkable. From the information she'd sent him, he knew Robbie had a mind that came along once in a lifetime. There was a time when Jeremy might have wondered what it would be like to help him explore his potential, to aid in his discovery of a universe most people never got to experience. That time had passed.

He looked up to find her watching him intently. He was used to being stared at but there was something about the way she examined him as if she could see into his mind.

Then the look vanished and she edged closer to watch him as he measured a combination of herbs and oils and added it to the mixture.

"I'm sure you understand what I'm talking about," she continued, in a different, almost conversational voice. "What was your childhood like? Was it difficult to be different from everybody else?"

The personal question startled him so much he sloshed the liquid he was stirring. It spattered with a sizzle onto the newspaper-covered counter. Her eyes widened and she stepped back.

Jeremy grinned, pleased with her reaction. "I told you to stay away."

"I don't take orders very well."

"No kidding?" He didn't have to be a genius to figure that out.

It was unusual for anyone to have the nerve—or the interest—to ask him such personal questions. Usually people saw what they wanted to see. "I don't think my childhood is any of your business."

"It is if you're thinking about helping me with Robbie."

"I'm not thinking about helping you with Robbie," he pointed out.

She ignored his point, and continued with her own. "I read an article about when you were eight years old. You had just won a 'War of the Brains' competition against people twice your age."

He remembered the day well. The reporters, the doubting professors, all wanting a look at the freak of nature.

She shook her head. "I couldn't even understand the question they asked you."

"Physics isn't an easy subject."

"Especially for an eight-year-old."

He thought he caught a glimpse of sympathy in her eyes.

"I would think it would be difficult to be put on display like that at such a young age."

"It was fine." If you considered it fine to be a lab rat.

"I haven't subjected Robbie to any of that kind of publicity. I've tried to keep him out of the public eye as much as possible."

He could commend her for that, at least. Allowing privacy to be one's self had been one of the principles his school had been founded on. "So you understand the need for solitude?" As long, he thought, as it didn't conflict with her own desires.

"Of course," she agreed. "Especially since others might get the wrong idea about someone with your abilities."

"The wrong idea?"

"They might find it strange, even weird, I suppose."

"Is that right?" he managed to say, the rein on his temper straining. "And what about you, Abby? What do you think about me?"

She'd been intently watching his proceedings, but now she looked away, appearing faintly embarrassed. "I haven't decided yet."

Her actions and words declared otherwise. She looked at him and saw the freak, the mutant. Her next comment confirmed it.

"I would think that someone who's lived through the kind of experiences you have would want to give something back instead of just wasting that knowledge."

Control snapped like the leash on a monster. He dropped the spoon which sank beneath the mixture and ripped the goggles from his eyes to stare at her. "What do you know about it? You couldn't understand what it's like!"

She didn't jump back. Or run screaming from his home. Instead she looked straight at him for the first time since they'd entered the house. He saw satisfaction, not revulsion, in those startling eyes.

"That's exactly my point," she said. "How could I? My childhood was filled with dolls and dress-up, not mathematic calculations. It's impossible for me to understand what it's like for my son—or for you. That's why I need your help."

It took an amazingly long time for Jeremy to realize he'd been conned. She'd been leading him to this conclusion all along. He had to respect the ingenuity. It was a sign of gifted intelligence to look at problems with originality and resourcefulness. Perhaps her son wasn't as different from her as she thought.

Because she was beginning to intrigue him, he filled his voice with firmness and finality. "I can't help you."

To his amazement, she looked shocked at his answer, as if she'd really expected him to change his mind. "Can't or won't?" she challenged.

"Can't *and* won't. I can suggest someone, a counselor," he said when she finally took a breath. "Maybe the two of you can see him together."

"I don't want a counselor," she insisted. "I want you."

Even knowing what she meant, her words lanced through him. "You don't understand what you're asking. Didn't you hear that I eat small children for breakfast?"

"That's not what some of your former students said."

He couldn't believe it. She'd shocked him again. "You contacted my students? What right do you have to...?"

"The rights of a mother. Do you think I would come all this way if I hadn't checked you out? My son's future is at stake!"

"Look, let's get this thing settled once and for all. I am not going to teach your son or any other child."

Abby frowned and Jeremy wondered if he had finally gotten through to her.

"I didn't ask you to," she responded. "I want you to teach me."

Chapter Three

"What are you talking about?" he asked. "You're not a genius."

Abby felt the heat rise on her face as he bluntly stated the obvious. "That's the point."

"What's the point?" he asked, obviously confused. "I thought you wanted me to enroll Robbie in my program?"

"That was never my intent. I hope you won't take this the wrong way, but I'm not sure you'd be a good influence on him." The last thing Robbie needed in his life right now was a twisted and scarred recluse as a role model.

He appeared stunned. "Then what *do* you want?"

"As I said, I want you to work with me." Although it galled her to confess it to this man, she knew he would accept nothing less than the truth. "I'm not smart enough to do this myself."

"To do what?"

"Decide Robbie's future. He can't attend a normal elementary school and the higher level schools won't take him. Obviously you'll agree that home schooling is not an option. How can I know what's best for my son? I don't have a Ph.D. or any of those other letters you have tacked on behind your name. I never even went to college, for heaven's sake."

"What has college got to do with anything?"

He sounded truly perplexed and she couldn't help wondering if it was a new experience for him. Join the club. "I didn't pay much attention in school," she admitted. "I was always too busy going to parties or hanging around with my friends to bother with anything as boring as studying."

"Do you think that if you'd paid attention in algebra, you'd have been prepared for someone with Robbie's intellect?"

She shrugged. "Maybe not, but I'd be a step closer. I was so sure that there'd be plenty of time to get serious." She took a deep breath and continued, determined to get it all out. "I met Robbie's father when I was only sixteen. He was older than me, already finishing college with top grades and expectations for a fast track to success. When he said we looked good together, I thought he meant we belonged together. We were married when I was just eighteen."

Jeremy listened to her story without expression. She wasn't even sure if he was actually listening, or if his mind had wandered off the way Robbie's sometimes did, until he responded. "Didn't your parents have anything to say about that?"

"We eloped. My parents were killed in an accident when I was young. I lived with my grandmother. Ted convinced me he had everything figured out and I believed him. Turns out, I was wrong."

"You were young. It's called immaturity. Most kids are like that."

The fact that he was defending her made her feel worse. "Were you?"

He shook his head. "Hardly."

Of course not. She tried to picture him skipping classes to go to the beach or spending his time studying the fine art of flirting, but she failed.

His eyes focused on a spot beyond her head and she could tell he was looking into the past. It didn't appear to be a comfortable place. "I'd have given just about anything to be able to have a normal, carefree childhood." As soon as the words left his mouth, he appeared shocked to have said them.

She got a mental picture of a young Jeremy, with his awkward clothes and remarkable brain. Had no one seen beyond those things, to the person inside? Was that how Robbie felt? It made her even more determined to figure out what he needed to be happy.

"At first everything was fine," she said. "Ted went to graduate school while I worked. He was smart and ambitious." And he'd made it clear that she shouldn't bother trying to understand the complicated life he'd mapped out for them. "Then Robbie came along and everything changed. We could see right from the beginning that he was different. At first Ted treated him like a trophy to be trotted out and placed on the mantel for friends to see, but then it started to become clear that Robbie's abilities far outmeasured Ted's and he began to see his own son as a threat. Ted just didn't seem to know what to do with him." It had been a shock to discover there wasn't much substance behind her husband's confident exterior.

"But you did?"

She laughed at the notion. "Sometimes I felt as helpless as if I was the infant, only there was no one to give me the answers or take care of me. I've been struggling to stay one step ahead of him ever since.'' Without meaning to, she stepped closer. ''He's my own son and I can't even understand what he's saying half the time. I've got two months to figure out what's best for his future and I'll do whatever it takes to help him.''

''You must be desperate if you've decided to center your plan around me.''

''I am.'' She didn't think she'd realized just how much was at risk before she'd met him.

Abby had expected him to be different. But dealing with Robbie had made her believe that she could deal with different. She'd known she would be asking a lot of a man whose solitary life wasn't exactly a secret, but for her son's sake she'd been willing to try.

But this awareness of him had caught her completely by surprise. She told herself it was a result of her attempts to find out about the man behind the brain, but there seemed to be something more basic, more dangerous, about her reaction to him. And she was very much afraid it had nothing to do with his mind.

Abby might not know much, but she knew anything deeper between them was out of the question. She had enough problems without allowing another superhuman into a life that was already too far from ordinary. Besides, if her husband had thought she was stupid, she could only imagine what Jeremy would think of her.

He'd turned to tend the mysterious concoction he was brewing, remaining silent for a long stretch of time before responding. ''For the sake of argument, let's just say that your frivolous teen years did contribute, marginally, to the difficulties you're facing now. Exactly what are you hoping to learn? Calculus for beginners? Quantum physics in twelve easy lessons?''

''I want to find out about you.''

His head bolted up. "You want to study me? What kind of aberration do you think I am?"

She stepped closer, only the counter separating them. "I think you're a man who looks at a rainbow and sees sunlight reflecting through little drops of water."

"Refracting," he corrected.

Abby shrugged, conceding the point, believing her own had just been made. "I see a spray of reds and blues and greens floating across the sky. I wonder what I'd do with a pot full of gold."

He looked bewildered by her response.

"I bet you fall asleep by adding columns of numbers in your head," she challenged.

"If I'm lucky."

Abby wondered what kinds of problems and anguish would keep a man like him awake. If they were anything like the nightmares that sometimes woke Robbie, they must be doozies. "You have experienced the kind of things Robbie is going through. You understand things I will never comprehend."

Jeremy stared deep into the murky brown liquid in front of him, no longer seeing the mixture's progress. Dear heaven, it was worse than he'd imagined. She did see him as a freak. Maybe they should put him in a cage and let children throw candy at his head.

Worse yet, when he looked across his kitchen at the stunningly beautiful woman observing him, his thoughts weren't the least bit cerebral. Desire was strong and real, and completely unacceptable.

"So you'd like to make me into your own personal guinea pig?"

"Of course not. I just want to ask you some questions, see what makes you happy, what you would have done differently if you'd had the chance."

She wanted to know what he would have done differently? He thought of the series of accidents and mistakes that had shaped his life. But the past didn't matter. Not even the most brilliant minds in the world had figured out a way to turn back time.

However, the future still waited for Robbie and others like him. Jeremy had once thought he could make a difference. He'd been wrong.

She seemed to mistake his brooding silence as a sign to continue. "If I'm going to enroll Robbie in the fall, I haven't got much time, so it wouldn't require much of a commitment from you," she explained, clearly having thought this out completely. "You wouldn't have to do anything, really, just be yourself and tell me what it's like."

"Is that all?" he asked dryly.

"Well, I suppose it might be a bit of an inconvenience from time to time. I figured, with all I have to learn, that I might have to be here quite a bit."

A bit of an inconvenience? He supposed that was one way of looking at things. "What possible reason would I have to agree to such an undertaking?"

"I understand that I'm asking a lot of you, but I'm not asking you to do it for free."

"You're planning to offer me a stipend for invading my life and dissecting it into little pieces?"

"Well, actually, I wouldn't be able to pay you, but I would be willing to trade services. Your talents in exchange for mine."

Because she was beginning to intrigue him, he made his expression purposely leering. "That's an interesting proposition. What exactly are your special talents?"

She gave no indication that she noticed his double meaning. "I'll clean your house for you."

"You'll do what?" he blurted. Her offer was the last thing he expected—or maybe the second to the last. The thought of her cleaning was almost too incredulous to be true. With those delicate features, dainty hands? "Sure you will."

"That's what I do. After my husband left, I discovered I didn't have the schooling to get a job good enough to support us. I was a waitress for a while. You'd be surprised by the kind of money you can make just serving people food."

Looking at her, Jeremy wasn't surprised at all. He imagined people would throw money at her to keep her coming back.

"But waitressing caused me to be away from Robbie too long and too late. So now I clean people's houses. It's the perfect solution. I can make my own hours and be around for Robbie. I can work anywhere, there's always somebody who needs help, and I'm good at what I do."

He could see that she'd given it a lot of thought, but he couldn't believe she'd chosen a path others would consider subservient. "What about your husband? Didn't he provide support?"

"I didn't want the strings he attached. He wanted me to send Robbie to boarding school, said he had the right to make the decisions if he was going to pay. I wasn't going to send my son away." She seemed to dare him to disagree. "We're doing fine on our own. I started out with only a few houses, but the business grew so much that I hired a whole fleet of other women to work with me. One of them is taking care of the company until I get back. If I have to leave Pittsburgh permanently because of Robbie, she wants to buy it from me."

She was serious. She was offering to do menial labor in exchange for his opening his life to her prying eyes. She had to know that if he had required domestic assistance he would have arranged it, yet she'd made the suggestion anyway, obstinately going after what she wanted in a way he could almost admire. He pictured the way she had examined his house so curiously before and realized her interest might have been more professional than personal, but that didn't change the facts. Like the rest of the world, she saw him as nothing more than a mutant specimen.

"Why me?" he couldn't help but ask. "There are a lot of smart people in the world. Most of them are better-adjusted than I am."

"You worked with kids. I figure you saw what worked, what made them fulfilled and happy."

"Not always," he answered, his voice grim as he thought about the past.

"But sometimes? Even if you've only discovered what doesn't work, you've already got a head start on everything I have to learn. You've been there. I can't begin to imagine what it's like."

"You might not want to know."

"I have to find out. Robbie's whole life depends on it. What if I make a mistake? What if I'm responsible for ruining his life because I made the wrong decision?"

The memory of one young face in particular swam across the swirl inside the pot. Leonard had been young when he'd first come to Jeremy's attention. Not much older than Abby's son was now. "You'd have to learn to live with it," he answered finally.

"I'm not willing to take that chance. He's my son. I have to do the right thing. He deserves that much at least."

Jeremy felt himself weakening. What she was asking was unthinkable, but if he agreed to be the subject in her little pet project he might actually be able to make a difference in one life. The potential of helping those whose intelligence made them different from others was what had prompted him to open Still Waters in the first place. He'd naively hoped to give those special children a place where they could feel normal, where they could explore their minds without drawing attention to their differences.

Eventually, he knew, her amazingly intelligent child would grow up to be nothing more than an extremely intelligent adult. But whether he survived the journey and thrived was still in question. She was giving Jeremy a chance to help without the risks that he would harm instead.

He reminded himself that was not his problem. But the part of him that had once thought that wisdom brought responsibility made him irate.

"Do you know how long it's been since I've been with a woman?" he asked abruptly.

She swallowed audibly. "No."

"It has been a very long time. If you'd like I could tell you down to the hours and minutes." He couldn't help but wonder if he was trying to talk her out of the bizarre scheme, or himself.

"I don't think that's the issue here."

"Which just goes to show what you know."

Trying to maintain his eroding common sense, he checked the mixture and found it ready. He strode past her, catching a hint of her scent, something clean and clear. It caused him to slam open the cabinet door where he'd stored a collection of odd-shaped boxes, pots and containers for this project. He lined the selection of items up along the counter, catching her bewildered expression from the corner of his eye.

"Do you understand what you're asking?" he asked. "You want to invade my life, pick it apart and use it to guide your son to a life completely different from my own?''

''Yes,'' she agreed, as if satisfied that he'd grasped the concept. He saw regret and perhaps pain in her gaze, but that didn't stop her. ''I'm not giving up, no matter what you say. This is too important.''

''And what if—*when*—I decline your offer?''

''Not even then. I'm planning to stick around whether you agree or not. I figure I can find out enough about you by asking around. I don't know what else to do.''

Jeremy took a deep breath and searched for logic. Whatever she lacked in higher intelligence—if anything—she certainly made up for in stubbornness. Of course, determination alone wouldn't be enough to sway him. He'd been known to go up against the entire academic community for something he believed in. Something like his students, for instance.

He believed her when she said she'd stick around until she got what she wanted. She'd hound him whether he agreed or not, making a nuisance of herself, reminding him of everything he could never have, and digging up a past that should remain buried.

Or he could chase her away the easiest way possible, by giving her what she wanted—a glimpse into the life of a brilliant misfit. She wouldn't last long.

If she truly wanted to help her son, she'd take what she saw and dedicate herself to making sure he turned out differently. In a roundabout way, maybe he could help the boy.

Or, at the very least, he wouldn't be able to hurt him.

''If I agree…''

She actually gave a little jump of joy into the air, causing Jeremy to regret his decision even before he'd finished making it. Who actually leaped for joy? he wondered.

There'd be no more leaping if he had anything to say about it.

He narrowed his eyes at her. "*If* I agree, there will be certain guidelines that have to be adhered to."

"Absolutely. Whatever you say. You won't be sorry."

He was already sorry. She was a beautiful woman under the worst of circumstances, but happiness actually made her glow. He was going to have to make sure that this association didn't last long. "The first, and most important rule, is that there are no children allowed. I will not work with your son, teach him, talk to him, or see him. Is that understood?"

"Hmm. I think I got the message."

He refused to be amused. "I hope so."

She managed to control her smile, a fact for which Jeremy was absurdly grateful. "Secondly, you may ask any questions you wish, but I may choose not to answer. Certain areas are off-limits. If you push, I will refuse any association in the future."

She nodded eagerly. "That sounds fair."

For some reason, he didn't believe her. But she'd find out he was serious soon enough if she tried to cross that line. Whatever problems Abby and her son faced, they weren't nearly as important to him as protecting his past mistakes from prying eyes.

Jeremy returned to the pan and observed the mixture inside. "It is time for me to continue with the next step of my project. I'm afraid you'll have to leave now."

"Sure. No problem." Now that she'd gotten what she'd come for, she seemed equally eager to depart. She'd headed toward the door, steps away from Jeremy's returned peace of mind, when she stopped suddenly. "Can I ask you one more thing before I leave?"

Jeremy sighed. "Why not?"

Apparently missing his sarcasm, she pointed to the pan he'd been tending all morning. "What are you making there, anyway?"

He'd been so sure she wouldn't ask. The fact that he'd miscalculated once again didn't bode well for their limited future together. "I am making soap," he admitted finally.

"Really?" She scanned the necessary chemicals, tools and molds, bewilderment and apprehension once again returning to her face. "I know you're a supergenius and all, but you know you can buy that stuff at the store, right?"

He glared at her with no obvious results. "I prefer to be self-reliant. I don't like to be around other people."

An awkward silence fell as they considered the implications of the coming weeks. "Don't worry," she assured him. "You'll hardly know I'm around."

They both knew she was mistaken.

Chapter Four

Dear God, she was singing!

Abby had invaded his house first thing this morning, bringing her piles of buckets and bottles, and cheerfully inquiring about which room he wanted her to start in. When he'd indicated—in what he considered a direct manner—that he didn't have a preference and that she could begin on the roof for all he cared, she'd scolded him about waking up on the wrong side of the bed and headed off to the first room she'd encountered, the formal front parlor.

He'd prepared himself for a barrage of nosy questions. In fact, one might say he'd been braced for war. According to his stratagem, he'd intended to set the tone early, giving her no opportunity to twist and wheedle her way into areas he had no intention of allowing her to explore. Instead she'd continued with the pretense of cleaning his house, somehow diffusing his careful plan.

And now this! Her off-tone voice seeped through the house, distracting him from any hope he might have had of getting some work done.

Jeremy slammed the cover on the journal he'd been trying to read. A person could only take so much! He wasn't going to let her get away with it. He was widely accepted as one of the most brilliant minds in the country. He could handle one self-admittedly simple young woman.

He strode into the living room, his remarks already forming on his lips, when he saw her. She'd probably thought he'd been joking when he'd mentioned his sexual drought and the effect having her in the house might have on him, but she'd have been wrong. Just the sight of her hit him with the impact of a punch to the solar plexus.

She'd pulled all of that glorious hair from her face and covered it with a bright blue bandanna. Shapeless overalls—obviously not intended to attract notice and failing— enveloped her body with the exception of her slim, deceptively strong arms. At the moment those arms were straining as she attempted to reach the top of one of the arched windows at the front of his house. With one foot stretched precariously on the windowsill and the other wriggling on an unsteady stepladder she'd brought with her, she was in the process of trying to unhook the heavy, dark drapes that had come with the house. At the same time, she continued doing her best to massacre some song whose lyrics seemed to consist of a repeated refrain of, "Do it to me, baby!"

"What are you doing?" he snapped.

At the sound of his voice, she swung in his direction, the momentum nearly having the effect of toppling her off the ladder. Jeremy actually saw her weave and falter, but he found himself incapable of moving. Thankfully she grasped the edge of his ornate drapes and righted herself before she came crashing to the ground.

Still, Jeremy remained frozen in place. What was wrong with him? He could calculate decimals to infinity, but when he'd been needed to react, his brain had simply malfunctioned. The failure just went to prove how inadequate he was to deal with normal people in normal situations.

"You startled me!" With her hand covering her breast, she stared at him as if afraid he might bite.

It was more of a concern than she might have wanted to believe.

A combination of fear for her safety and his own attraction made his voice sharp. "Maybe if you hadn't been...singing," he made it clear that he used the term lightly, "you'd have heard me when I came in."

The lighthearted, relaxed demeanor she'd been exhibiting before she realized he was in the room vanished, to be replaced with a more guarded expression. He should have been used to it, yet somehow, after all these years of people reacting to him that way, it still managed to hurt.

"I'm sorry. Did I disturb you?"

In any number of ways, he thought.

Her heavy lashes lowered to conceal her expression when his silence answered her question. "I hope you don't mind. I was just trying to take down these curtains so that I could wash the windows. I'm going to air them out for a while, if that's okay with you." She seemed braced for criticism.

Jeremy didn't disappoint her, still caught up with the notion of yet another person hurting themselves because of him. Not to mention the idea of what he'd have done if he'd had the ability to move and she'd fallen into his arms. "I told you before, I don't care what you do."

"I guess I'll take that as a yes." Turning away from him, she returned to her task of trying to raise the heavy dowel that held the drapes in place. "This is a great room," she ventured hesitantly. "It's got such character."

Jeremy gratefully accepted the bid to look elsewhere, glancing around the room as if seeing it for the first time.

On the opposite end of the room from the windows, a stone fireplace served as the focal point. The mahogany mantel now glowed as a result of her efforts, as did the Tiffany chandelier in the center of the room. An assortment of wing chairs were scattered around the room, making it a perfect location for what had previously been known as the debate room. He remembered his own pride and satisfaction when his students had battled over ideas and solutions.

He'd once been so optimistic about their opportunity to change the future and make the world a better place with their unique abilities. What a fool he'd been.

"You know, this wallpaper is silk," she said, breaking him free of the memories. "It's in great condition. I think the only thing making this room gloomy is the drapes." She tugged again without success at the pole holding them in place.

Jeremy knew just how depressing the window coverings were. He'd been the one to draw them shut, closing out the outside world and his own pain when he'd heard about Leonard and shut down the school for good.

"I think it would look much nicer if you took these down and put up something bright. A floral pattern, maybe."

"You want me to cover my windows with flowers?"

She looked over at his frowning face and seemed to reconsider. "I suppose you're right. Dark and dreary might be more appropriate."

He was pretty sure he'd just been insulted, but he couldn't be sure. Was that how she saw him? Dark and dreary? He supposed that was a close enough description. At least she hadn't added dangerous or demented. Though she probably would before they were through.

She'd turned back to her pursuit of removing the material, still having no success. The drapes might not be the most aesthetically pleasing in the world, but they were well made and suited the rest of the decor. It was why he hadn't changed them when he'd bought the house from the original owner. Jeremy knew their weight would make them nearly impossible for her to handle herself, yet even though he was standing right there she still made no move to ask for help. He finally gave up waiting for her common sense to kick in and crossed the room to assist her.

When he dragged over a heavy wooden chair and climbed up onto it, she looked so shocked he feared she might nearly fall off the ladder again.

"The trouble," he explained, "is that your center of gravity is very high and you are not utilizing your body strength effectively."

"Plus these suckers are really heavy," she added.

"True." He turned his face away so that she wouldn't see the smile that twisted his lips without his consent. He didn't want her to get the wrong idea that he still had a sense of humor. "Let's lift together and see if we can get them free. On the count of three?" He gave the order in a form of a question.

She frowned and rolled her eyes pensively. "I think I can manage that."

Jeremy pressed his lips together to keep from grinning. "Let's find out," he said. "One. Two. Three."

Together they lifted and the dowel slipped from its holder. Sunlight streamed into the room, causing him to blink as they lowered the drapes. The brightened room only served to highlight Abby all the more as she stood grinning with satisfaction at the window. She clearly hadn't taken any pains with her appearance, unless it was to try to hide her attractiveness, but if that was her objective, she'd failed miserably. She couldn't conceal the flawless skin, the full sensual mouth, the eyes glowing with enthusiasm for a task most would consider mundane.

He imagined her shock if she knew the direction his thoughts were taking, in full, detailed images. She probably considered him too cerebral to feel desire, but she'd be wrong. Despite his other attributes, he was still a man.

"Have you got any old newspapers?" she asked, obviously unaffected by any similar longing.

Jeremy turned back to the window, hoping she hadn't caught him staring. "Is it time for a break already?"

"Oh, no. I was going to use them to clean the windows. I brought paper towels, but newspapers actually work much better."

"I know that. I was joking," he explained, embarrassed that he'd been so preoccupied that he hadn't had the presence of mind to stop the slip.

She blinked owlishly. "You were...? Oh!"

Obviously he was out of practice. It was a good thing he hadn't told her the one about the physicist and the isosceles triangle. Nobody ever laughed at that one. "There's a pile of papers in the library. Help yourself."

Abby used the excuse to escape his perceptive gaze, telling herself not to rush from the room. What was it about him that made her feel so on edge when he was around? It wasn't the beastly attitude he used to try to scare her away. If he hoped to cower her into retreat, she intended to disappoint him.

And it couldn't be the effect of his simmering magnetism. Very early in life, she'd mastered the technique of dealing with the opposite sex. "Just treat them as if they are human," she'd told her friends who envied the way she'd attracted boys as much as her ability to discourage their attention without hurting their feelings.

But there was something about Jeremy that didn't allow

her to maintain that distance. He knew it, too. In fact, he seemed to know everything. She wished she could ask him to explain it to her. Then she'd understand why a simple attempt at humor—an awkward attempt, at that—had left her tongue-tied and staring stupidly. And why she'd attacked the house like a cleaning machine when she'd finally had a chance to ask the questions she so needed to know. And why she'd spent the night thinking about how lonely it must be in that big old house. And why she had the persistent, nagging notion that somehow she might be able to help him as much as he helped her.

That was just the kind of lopsided logic that had driven her ex-husband crazy. Jeremy hadn't given her any indication that he wanted anything from her besides her absence. If there was one lesson she should have learned from her marriage it was that a man like him would never have anything in common with a woman like her. If she had any sense, she'd remember that.

Abby crossed the hall to the library she'd discovered earlier that morning. It was a huge two-story room with books from floor to ceiling, and a balcony circling the room to allow access to the higher books. The woodwork was warm and rich, not dark like the rest of the house, as if this room had been remodeled. Cozy chairs and couches were scattered throughout.

She moved closer, looking at the array of books. She couldn't even understand the titles of some of the journals, but there was also an impressive collection of fictional classics as well as modern bestsellers. She'd begun to reach for a dog-eared horror story, one of her favorites, when she heard him coming down the hall. She slipped it back into place.

"There you are. I thought you might have gotten lost."

So much for his judgment of her abilities. "No, I found it. I was just looking at all the books."

He glanced around and she thought she might have detected a glimmer of pride. "I love to read. Books give you so much without expecting anything in return."

Unlike people, she thought, who had apparently asked so much of him and given so little back. Abby would have liked to respond. It was the first personal comment he'd made since she'd met him. But she didn't know what to say.

He didn't seem to need a reply. "You can borrow any of these books while you're here."

Abby reached up and chose a book at random. She looked down at the title. "Great, I've been meaning to catch up on the Theories and Practices of Mathematical Logic."

His lips twisted into something resembling a grin. She was almost sure of it.

"I was thinking more about this section over here," he pointed out. "I've got an extensive collection of books on gifted children."

She crossed the room and looked at the titles. Some, she'd already read in her attempts to find out all she could about Robbie's situation. Others looked more like scientific studies that she was sure she wouldn't be able to decipher. One book in particular caught her eye.

"My Life as a Brain," she read. "By Jeremy Waters."

"I wanted to call it, *My Life as a Freak,* but the editors thought that was too negative."

Was that the way he saw himself? As a freak? Would Robbie grow up to feel the same way? Not if she had anything to say about it, she promised herself.

She took the book from the shelf, trying to imagine accomplishing enough in your life to write about. "I found out about your book in one of the articles I read about you," she said with awe, "but I hadn't been able to find a copy."

"I'm sure it's out of print by now. I wrote it a long time ago and even then it wasn't exactly a big seller."

She flipped open to the inside cover and saw the picture of a very young Jeremy. He'd been only a boy when he'd written it, she realized, maybe fifteen or sixteen years old. He'd begun to outgrow the awkwardness of his famous youth and taken on the roughly handsome traits he'd grown into, staring into the camera with open defiance she'd come to recognize.

She scanned the caption below his picture and read that the book was about surviving life after early notoriety. At the age of fifteen, he made it seem as if his life was already over. She couldn't wait to find out what had made him feel that way, what had shaped him to be the man he had become. And she could admit, if only to herself, that some of her reasons had nothing to do with her son.

"Do you mind if I borrow this?" she asked. Although he'd already offered, she half expected him to snatch it out of her hands in an attempt to protect his carefully guarded privacy.

Instead he shrugged. "It's not a pretty story, but if it will answer some of your questions and get you out of here sooner, then help yourself."

Abby didn't take offense, looking past his crankiness to the offer behind it. "Thank you."

He bristled even more. She expected to see the hair stand up on his arms, the way an animal's does when it's feeling threatened. He didn't like it when people got too close. What would happen if someone got inside that shell of his? she wondered.

"I didn't do anything yet," he grumbled. "If you are

going to insist on intruding in my life, why don't you get started so I can finally get some work done around here?''

This was the chance she'd been waiting for. Abby had hundreds, thousands, of questions she wanted to ask him. So why did she suddenly feel so nervous about sitting down with him to talk? ''The windows—''

''Can wait. They're not going anywhere, and apparently neither are you until you get what you've come for. Let's get this over with.''

''All right,'' she responded. ''Do you want to work in here?''

''Is there something wrong with this room?'' he asked with annoyance.

On the contrary, it seemed too cozy, too intimate. Abby decided not to mention it. ''Of course not. This will be fine.''

''What a relief,'' he drawled, not sounding relieved at all. He sat on the couch and she chose a seat in a chair opposite him, not realizing how close they were until their feet almost tangled. She could see his eyes, narrowed in a way she knew he thought to be intimidating, but too direct and intense to be successful. His collared shirt was starched and stiff, but it couldn't hide the strength of his shoulders. She wondered what drove him to build his body in such a physical way, when his mind was already so extraordinary. Then she remembered that his body was none of her concern. It was his mind she had to concentrate on.

Luckily that mind couldn't read hers. ''What do you want to know?'' he asked.

She took a deep breath and tried to focus. ''Okay. Let me start with something easy. Why did you decide to open Still Waters?''

He folded his arms across his chest. "The subject of the school is off-limits."

It seemed this wasn't going to be quite as easy as she'd hoped. Why wasn't she surprised? "You said I could ask whatever I wanted," she reminded him.

"I also told you I wouldn't answer questions on certain subjects. The school is one of them."

"Why?" she persisted. "It seems like a relevant subject to me. I'm trying to figure out what kind of school to send my son and you started a school designed to help kids with his abilities."

"The school is closed now. It doesn't matter."

"But you opened it in the first place because you saw a need. What did you hope to accomplish?"

He didn't respond and she realized he wasn't going to. *Hmmp!* And people called her stubborn. Not willing to give up, she changed the direction of her questions. "All right. We'll forget about the school for now. How about your theories of the best way to deal with child prodigies? What works and what doesn't?"

"I'd rather not talk about my theories," he told her.

She stared at him. "You don't want to talk about what you've learned in working with young geniuses?"

"No."

Abby nodded slowly, but anyone who knew her wouldn't have confused the gesture with agreement. "No theories. Got it." She leaned back in the chair, settling in to stay for a while. "How about your first car? What color was it?"

Jeremy frowned. "Silver. It was electric and I made it myself. What does that have to do with anything?"

"Nothing. I just wanted to find a question you would answer."

"I'm not trying to be difficult," he told her.

"Why try when it comes so easily?" she snapped, her patience at an end. "What are you trying to hide? Your life's an open book." She lifted the written proof.

"I'm not trying to hide anything." His voice had become quiet, more lethal than she'd heard it before. "Maybe I'm just sick of being treated like a science experiment."

"Is that what you think I'm doing? I assure you my reasons are much more personal. At this stage in his life, my five-year-old son has a few, simple goals. He plans to travel to Mars at his earliest opportunity, be a nuclear physicist and find the cure for cancer."

Jeremy nodded. "Sounds reasonable."

"And maybe *you* could have been the one to find that cure, but instead you chose to teach a select group of kids just like you. Why?"

"Perhaps I wanted to start a society of masterminds and rule the world."

"I don't think so."

"How could you possibly know what I was thinking?" His tone was filled with mockery and derision.

Abby withstood the direct hit of his insult, a flashback to how her husband used to handle all of their discussions. Especially the ones in which she had a valid point. He'd hated allowing her to get the upper hand and would always bring up her lack of education and intellect when arguing. Abby had learned not to bother with the fight, simply following the most direct route to get what she wanted with dogged determination. For Robbie's sake, she plowed on now. What Jeremy thought of her personally was unimportant.

"I may not know what you were thinking, but I can guess."

He shook his head, clearly amused. "And when we're

done with that game, we can play Pin the Tail on the Donkey.''

''I'd rather stick with Twenty Questions.''

''Go ahead,'' he responded. ''Do you want to know if it's animal, vegetable, or mineral?''

''I want to know if you opened your school because you were trying to help. I think you saw a need that nobody else could fill.''

She saw his shock at her suggestion, and knew she was right by the flash of pain that was quickly banked. ''What I was trying to do doesn't matter.''

''It does to me.''

He slammed his hand down on the table beside him. The sound rang through the room like a gunshot. ''You want to know why I started the school?'' He didn't wait for an answer. ''I started it to keep those kids from becoming a freak like me.''

The outburst startled Abby into silence. It occurred to her, somewhat belatedly, that she'd miscalculated Jeremy's ferociousness. Despite his ill-tempered behavior since she'd met him, she'd considered his actions to be a method of keeping people away rather than a real personality trait. Now she realized she'd seen only a portion of his anger. As fearsome as the display was, he managed to control it.

Jeremy shook his head, regaining his composure with obvious effort. He didn't say anything for a long time. She wasn't sure he was going to talk to her again. When he did speak, it was in a quiet, defeated voice. ''I just wanted the kids to fit in. I wanted them to have a childhood. I wanted them to have fun.''

As much as Jeremy's outburst had startled Abby, this declaration shocked her to the core. Without realizing she'd moved, she rose and sat next to him. She wasn't sure why she felt the need. He certainly hadn't asked for her to cross the chasm that separated them with more than distance. He didn't require her closeness or her understanding.

"Damn it! I knew this was a mistake," he said when he saw the tears that had beaded in her eyes. "I'm sorry. I knew I shouldn't have said anything."

She grabbed his hand and clung. "No, it's not that. It's just that nobody has ever said that to me before, about wanting the kids to be kids, no matter how smart they are."

He shook his head, the face that had been so angry only moments ago, now filled with remorse. He placed his hand on her shoulder, in support and apology. "I wasn't thinking. There's no reason to believe that Robbie will have any kind of problems like that."

Abby leaned toward him, allowing herself to absorb his strength. She stared into his eyes, looking for something to cling to and was surprised to find what she was looking for. "But that's just it. Since the moment Robbie was born, I've been waiting and listening and learning. All anyone ever sees is the fact that he's different. Nobody ever talks about him like he's a little boy."

They were so close, she could see those eyes widen with awareness and understanding as he realized she wasn't upset by what he'd said. Without being aware of it, his hand had begun to make circles on her back, awkward tender movements that were sending tendrils of longing through her.

Her voice was as soft as a whisper as she continued. "They tell me how to make the most of his potential, or how different he is. They don't get it."

"No, they don't," he agreed tightly.

Though they had nothing in common, they seemed to reach an understanding between them, however fragile.

"Just because someone is different doesn't mean they don't have the same needs as everyone else. The need to be loved, and to be happy." She realized she was staring at his mouth as if she would find the answers there.

"It's not that easy."

It wasn't the answer she wanted. "But it's possible, isn't it?" She reminded herself that they were talking about Robbie, about his future, not their own.

"Anything is possible." As if to prove it, he moved closer and his mouth touched hers, partly in apology, it seemed, and partly as if he couldn't stop himself. She didn't pull away, pressing against his lips with her own. They were softer than she'd expected, more pliant. It was her last logical thought before reason fled as he kissed her with abandon, no indication of his superbrain in evidence. There was just emotion and desire, barely repressed. She met the call with her own deeply buried hunger. How long had it been since she'd felt this way? Wanted and wanting? Maybe never.

Her arm wound around his neck. His hands gripped her waist. Their heads moved together, tilting in opposite directions to allow better access. He nipped at her bottom lip and her eyes opened to look directly into his.

Jeremy pulled away suddenly, gasping for breath. The action reminded her that she also needed oxygen and she pulled some into her lungs.

She couldn't think. Couldn't speak. Only her nerve endings seemed to be working—but they were suffering from overload. He seemed similarly struck.

For some reason, despite the intimacy they had just shared, it became important that he not realize how stunned she'd been by their kiss. It wouldn't look good if he knew that at the moment she didn't have a single logical thought in her head. After struggling to remember what they'd been talking about before he kissed her, she finally recalled his theory about dealing with genius kids. "So did it work?"

"Did what work?" He sounded confused, dazed, much the same way she felt herself. She had a feeling it wasn't a reaction he experienced often.

"Your theories on treating kids like they were normal?"

His hand stopped its hypnotic circle and Jeremy eased back. "I..."

His gaze suddenly changed, appearing haunted instead of stunned.

"What is it? What did I say? Did your theories work out?"

He'd moved only a few inches away, but suddenly Abby felt as if miles separated them. He hesitated so long she was sure he wasn't going to answer. Finally he nodded. "Yes, of course. Everything worked out fine."

Abby smiled. She'd known it. She was tempted to throw her arms around him again, but he got up from the couch. If everything was right, why did she suddenly feel as if something were very wrong?

Chapter Five

"Isn't it a beautiful day?" Abby asked Robbie as they headed toward the camp's drop-off area. The sun was shining, the birds chirped in the trees. And for the first time in as long as she could remember, she'd begun to envision a fulfilling future for her son. She had Jeremy to thank for that—only one of the surprises from the previous week that still had her reeling.

"It was seventy-six degrees when we left the apartment," Robbie reported, using a more analytical method to describe the conditions. "I set up a weather station outside my window."

"I noticed." She looked to the sky for her own method of evaluation. "Well, it doesn't look like we'll get any rain today. What do you have planned?"

Robbie shrugged. "At eight-fifteen we have instructional swim, followed by arts and crafts at nine-thirty. Yesterday I made a replica of the great pyramid out of macaroni. It wasn't to scale, of course."

"Of course."

Robbie's steps slowed as they got closer to the main building. Maybe, she thought, he was enjoying these moments of togetherness as much as she was.

"Are you going back to Dr. Waters's house today?" Robbie asked. He'd become fascinated by the man and grilled her for details each day when she picked him up at camp. "What are you planning to do there?"

"Oh, you know, the same old thing. Clean Dr. Waters's house." Pick Dr. Waters's brain. In the past several days, she'd poked and prodded, gaining little tidbits of valuable wisdom which he guarded as if he didn't have enough to spare.

"Maybe I should go along to keep you company," he offered.

"Oh, honey, that's sweet of you, but you don't have to do that. You just stay here and have some fun. You can tell me all about it when I come to pick you up tonight." Besides, Abby hadn't forgotten Jeremy's strict rules about not bringing Robbie. They'd definitely entered new ground with that mind-blowing kiss, but she didn't think she should push it.

He was still so full of contradictions, blindly passionate one minute and chillingly withdrawn the next. She wasn't sure what she'd expected from the brilliant Dr. Waters, but it certainly hadn't been barely controlled desire, masterful technique, or that thing he'd done with his tongue. He hadn't read that in any book.

"Go ahead," she told Robbie, when they'd reached the meeting spot for his group. "I'll see you tonight."

She bent down to give him a kiss, surprised when he wrapped his arms around her neck for a crushing hug. Abby held him tight, not caring what the other kids might think about the open display of affection. He might be destined for future greatness, but he was still her little boy.

Robbie finally pulled away and, after one final glance over his shoulder, joined the assembled group. A boy who looked much larger than Robbie greeted him with what appeared to be a friendly punch in the arm. Abby smiled. That's what he needed—a little male bonding.

Abby heard someone call her name and saw the camp's owner, Drew Danforth, headed her way. He was a good-looking man, she noted objectively, though Abby was sure she related to those attributes differently than most people. He wasn't responsible for the wavy brown hair or perfect smile any more than she had earned her looks or Robbie, his brain. It was what was inside that really mattered.

"Mrs. Melrose! Abby. I'm glad I caught you." His smile was set on stun, but she didn't hold it against him. "I wanted to see how you were doing."

"We're making progress, thanks. How is Robbie fitting in at camp?"

"He's doing fine, for the most part," Drew reported, his smile dimming a bit in an attempt, she was sure, to appear more professional. "There are the normal adjustments, of course, but nothing you need to worry about."

She watched Robbie's group as it lined up and began to file in the direction of the pool. Robbie was now chatting with yet another boy, this one with bright red hair, while the one she'd seen earlier was roughhousing with others at the end of the line. She sighed with relief. Although she'd tried to hide it, she'd been so worried that it wouldn't work out. It was a relief to know he was fitting in—just like Jeremy had described.

"It's not easy to handle a child alone, is it?" Drew asked, breaking into her thoughts. "Especially a child as unique as Robbie. Maybe it would do you some good to get out and let someone take care of you for a change."

Abby's attention snapped back to Drew. If she hadn't

been so preoccupied with thoughts of someone else, she'd have seen that coming. She didn't want anyone taking care of her. She wanted someone who could accept her while allowing her to take care of herself. She'd yet to find anyone who could fill that role. "I appreciate the offer," she responded, "but I need to concentrate on Robbie right now."

"I understand, but it wouldn't hurt to get out and have some fun, would it?"

She thought of Jeremy again, and the kiss that had been miles away from fun. It had sparked something long forgotten inside her, something she'd have been just as happy to remain dormant. And while he'd offered hope for Robbie's future, there was no chance for their own. She couldn't forget that.

Getting ideas about a personal involvement with Jeremy would be a mistake, but so would allowing Drew to get the wrong idea. "I appreciate the offer, but I've got too much on my plate right now." She glanced at her watch. "In fact, I should be getting to work now," she informed him politely.

Drew frowned with the confusion of someone unaccustomed to rejection. "Robbie told me you've been doing some work for Jeremy Waters," he said before she could escape. "Is that right?" His tone suggested her son must have made a mistake.

"I am," she confirmed, supposing he had reason to be shocked. "He's been giving me some advice on Robbie's future."

"And you're taking it?"

"Why wouldn't I?"

He shrugged, obviously hesitant to say anything more. "It's just that Dr. Waters has a certain reputation around here." Though they were surrounded by groups of boisterous children, Drew's voice lowered with concern and caution. "He has a habit of disappointing those who rely on him. Occasionally the results have been disastrous."

"What do you mean?" she asked.

"Just be careful around him," Drew cautioned. "He's different from the rest of us."

Abby couldn't dispute the evidence she'd seen of Jeremy's uniqueness. Yet, she'd begun to think she'd seen something else, too. Some connection between them that went beyond the physical. Not brainpower, of course. She could never hope to measure up there. But expectations. People had always looked at her and expected a certain kind of behavior. She thought his experience might be similar. Neither of them had ever had the chance to break free of the box people put them in. For all their differences, she'd thought for a moment there that they'd been able to understand each other.

But maybe she'd been wrong. Maybe there had been nothing between them but neglected hormones and a misguided attraction.

Either way, Abby reminded herself, it didn't make any difference. She was there to do a job and she wasn't going to let anything—not even that mind-numbing kiss—get in her way.

There were fresh flowers on his table. His kitchen floor had discovered the fountain of youth. She even did windows, leaving him a clear view to the outside world.

She had to be stopped.

She'd invaded his life with her questions and her comments, poking her nose in where it wasn't wanted, bringing up memories better left forgotten, refusing to take "absolutely not" for an answer.

He'd been so sure that after that kiss she'd have realized

what a disastrous mistake this scheme of hers had been. Yet she returned each day, scouring her way through his house and his head, and leaving him in a state of constant frustration.

Jeremy felt as though his brain was going to explode.

Abby would probably want to examine the contents.

When he heard her car rattle up his driveway and realized he'd been waiting expectantly for the sound, he decided something had to be done. He charged out of his house before she'd even come to a complete stop, determined to put an end to this madness before it was too late.

"What are you doing here?" He'd have assumed yesterday's debacle with his childhood scrapbook would have given her enough material to dwell on, but apparently she still hadn't delved deeply enough. What was next? The Rorschach Test or dental records?

She barely glanced at him as she got out of the car. "I assume that's one of those rhetorical questions. Like 'where do we come from?' or 'what's the meaning of the universe?' I've never been very good at those."

"No, I mean why do you keep coming back here?"

She shrugged, opening the rear door of her car and removing a mop and a bucket. "You don't think the house is finished, do you? I know we made good progress on that dining room yesterday but there is a lot left to do."

"I'm not talking about cleaning the house. I'm talking about..." His words trailed off as he wondered why he had to explain. That kiss between them had registered on the Richter scale and should have sent her running as far and as fast away from him as she could. It was an anomaly for his emotions to supercede his logic, but he'd lost all sense of judgment that day, responding to her with no more control than a randy teenager. Afterward, with his head still filled with her, he'd attempted to figure out what had happened, but no hypothesis had presented itself.

She returned to the back seat to retrieve a handled plastic tray filled with an assortment of cleaning supplies, which she placed on the ground next to the mop.

This was a mistake. He'd known it from the beginning. He shouldn't have let her even this close. He'd lied to her when he'd told her everything would be all right, and she had no reason to doubt him. By giving her false hope, he might have already done irreparable harm.

Life would never be normal for him. It might never work out right for Robbie. Certainly it would never again be all right for his former student, Leonard.

And it could never work out between the two of them. He couldn't forget that again.

She'd disappeared inside the car to get more supplies. Jeremy averted his gaze from her posterior wiggling with the effort. "This isn't going to work," he declared.

Her head smacked against the door frame when she jolted. Wincing, she threaded her hand through the cloud of hair and rubbed the tender spot. But he knew the pain in her eyes came from his announcement more than the bump.

"Is there something specific you're not satisfied with? I think the house is coming along nicely."

"It's not that. You're doing a great job…" The house almost looked like a home again. That was part of the problem.

"Oh good. I really liked the way the floors came out. I buffed them, did you notice? That oak is beautiful. It's hard to find that kind of workmanship today." She turned back toward the car, obviously intending to gather more supplies.

"I'm not talking about the damn floor," he snapped. "It

sparkles! I'm talking about the rest of it. About this crazy idea of yours. About us.''

Had he said us? That was a mistake. There was no us.

"I know what you're talking about."

He noticed the defensiveness of her tone and realized he'd heard it before when she thought he was being condescending. Yet from the way she was looking at him, direct and insightful, he became aware that she'd known what he'd been going to say all along. He was beginning to think she knew so much more than she gave herself credit for.

"Then why were you chattering about floors?"

"Because you obviously had a bee in your bonnet from the moment I got here."

"A bee in my…?"

"You're the one who suggested that geniuses should be treated like normal people. When Robbie throws a tantrum like that, the best thing to do is ignore it until he gets over it."

His eyes narrowed. "Did you just compare me to your five-year-old son? Because I'm pretty sure I could prove otherwise if you've forgotten."

The reminder of their close encounter was the last thing he'd intended to bring up and just went to show how much she affected his thought process, but it seemed to have the desired effect. Her gaze dropped to his mouth and a blush reddened her skin.

Her voice wasn't quite as motherly when she continued. "The point is that you're upset because I'm getting too close. You feel threatened. I believe, after reading your book, that it's a trait you developed very young. I blame your parents for not being there for you. I hope you don't take offense but they should have had their heads examined."

Jeremy blinked. "Since my parents are both professors with their doctorates at a very prestigious university, their heads have probably been examined quite often."

"Well, I'll bet they didn't get any degrees in common sense. If they had accepted you for what you were, maybe you wouldn't have had to keep proving yourself and setting impossibly high standards for yourself."

Jeremy attempted to assess her incredibly outrageous comments and concluded with a shock that she just might be right. When he'd written his book he'd made sure it didn't reflect badly on his parents despite the fact that he'd already had years to deal with being treated more like a trophy than a beloved child. It was another reason he'd opened Still Waters. He'd wanted those children to be accepted unconditionally. But he'd never admitted that fact to anyone.

Somehow, Abby had been able to detect his carefully hidden emotions. He'd never met anyone who understood human nature as well as she did.

But her perceptiveness wasn't the point. "Why are we talking about my parents?"

She looked him directly in the eye, not bothering to hide her feelings. "Because I don't want you to tell me I can't come back here," she stated bluntly. "I thought we were doing so well together."

It was clear that her opinion of their time together was very different from his. "You don't understand," he said, his frustration showing. "This is a very complicated situation."

There it was again, the narrowed gaze and braced stance of hers that seemed to be hurt and insistent at the same time.

"Why don't you try to explain it to me then?" she said.

He might as well just tell her the truth and get it over

with. She'd be hurt by what he had to say but it was better than giving her false hope. "I may not have been completely clear with you the other day when I implied that I had all the answers."

She leaned a hip against her car. "Funny, I don't recall you voluntarily providing any answers at all."

"It was after we…" No, he didn't want to bring that up again. "When I said that everything about my plan had worked out exactly as I'd hoped. That wasn't exactly true. It might have been the opposite of the truth, in fact."

"Are you saying it's impossible to lead a happy life if you happen to be smarter than most people?"

"Of course not." Why did she always twist his words? "Many child geniuses go on to live happy and productive lives." But some didn't. Nobody knew that better than he did. "If you're not like other people, they can make it difficult for you to fit in. It isn't always a comfortable life, despite the advantages."

"And you think this concept is too foreign for me to understand?" Her voice was laced with disappointment.

He didn't answer her question directly. She couldn't possibly comprehend the strain of constant rejection, the struggle to conform, the burden of knowledge you carried alone. "I think you're trying to do what's best for your son, but you need to try to see things from his perspective."

"I already admitted that I can't," she said. "I can't know what he knows. I can't see what you both see. I will never be able to fit into your world."

Jeremy absorbed the pain that came from her admission, even as he felt the shock that he could still be hurt. Hearing her state the obvious shouldn't have had the ability to wound him. He'd known it all along.

"But in some ways your life isn't so different from what

I faced," she continued. "I was the prettiest girl in school, the one everyone wanted to date, the one everyone wanted to be seen with."

"Is that your argument for identifying with my life?" he said with heavy sarcasm. It proved exactly the opposite, in fact. He'd been the one nobody wanted to date, nobody wanted to be seen with. And, as he recalled, the good-looking popular group had been the most brutal.

"Maybe not, but my point is that nobody ever really took the time to get to know me. They saw what they thought they saw. They never bothered to look deeper, to find out if there was something more than a pretty shell. They never gave me a chance."

"That's not the same." But he could see how someone as strong and smart as Abby might resent being typecast as a bubble-headed blonde. He supposed he'd been guilty of the same thing.

"I know that, but I'm saying I can understand how it might have felt for you when they didn't bother to look deeper than how you think. I think they missed the fact that you're harder on yourself than any bully could ever be. I think there's more to you than a brilliant reclusive outcast."

"You're wrong," he said. "That's exactly what I am." He had to make sure she understood that fact before they went any further. She could claim to understand him—and maybe, if he was honest with himself, she came closer than anyone he could remember—but if she thought there was going to be one of her cheerful rainbows at the end of this rainy season, she was mistaken.

"All right. Come in. I just hope you're not sorry."

Even as he said the words, Jeremy knew it was already too late for him.

As she followed him into the house, Abby hoped she wouldn't be sorry, too. Now that she'd gotten what she wanted, she couldn't be sure if her reaction was one of excitement or dread. She'd been so sure he was going to force her to leave, but instead he was inviting her in, allowing her a glimpse of the real Jeremy Waters. So far, the impressions she'd managed to gather had been hard-earned and surface deep, especially since the kiss. It was amazing how a man as commanding and magnetic as Jeremy could manage to become so invisible. Now that he was about to reveal himself, she wasn't sure she wanted to know.

She was certain her ex-husband would have had something to say about that kind of thinking.

However, she had better things to do than to worry about what Ted might have thought about this latest foolishness—like trying to keep up with the genius who was striding through his house as if he was being chased by demons. Without a backward glance to see if she was following, he made his way through the maze of rooms that she still hadn't managed to figure out. Abby hurried her steps to avoid being left behind.

Finally he entered one of the drearier rooms at the end of a corridor and stopped in front of a door that was nearly masked by the matching wall molding. Jeremy hesitated at the opening as if having second thoughts.

What did he keep hidden away in this secret spot? What was so advanced, so complex that he felt it would explain his way of life? Although this was what she'd come here for, she was suddenly afraid she might discover a world even more overwhelming than what she already faced, one she had no hope of ever sharing with Robbie.

Then he opened the door and it was too late for doubts. Sunlight flooded into the room, making her blink from the sudden contrast to the dark interior. She followed him over the threshold to what might have once been a porch but had been transformed to a greenhouse. The air was thick and humid, reminding Abby of a tropical rain forest exhibit where she had once taken Robbie. Every breath brought a barrage of scents from perfumed floral to earthy and sensual. Rows of tables filled the room, leaving very little space to navigate, and held an array of brightly colored exotic-looking plants.

"You grew all of these?" Even as the words left her mouth, she realized it was a stupid question, but she was awed by the assortment of greenery in front of her. One variety had huge, heart-shaped leaves of snowy-white, while another held bold stalks of crimson flowers that appeared somehow sexual.

She was surprised when he responded to the question despite its absurdity. "I am responsible for the cultivation of this compendium of artificially fertilized vegetation."

Her eyebrows rose at his description of the beautiful array of greenery. "I guess I'll take that as a yes." She wandered down the aisle, taking in the amazing assortment of plants, some carefully secluded, others sprouting out of water troughs instead of soil.

"You wanted to know what it's like to be a genius?"

Abby pulled her gaze away from one bush with blossoms of different colors. "Yes, I think it's important for Robbie's sake." And that was the only reason, she reminded herself.

"I don't sleep much, four hours or so if I'm lucky, and I spend hours wandering through the dark house alone."

"In this house?" She shuddered dramatically. "I don't know if you're brave or crazy."

He didn't respond to her attempt at humor, continuing in a tone as gloomy as the haunted mansion he called home. "I can go weeks or months without talking to another person."

On that, at least, she could relate. The feelings of isolation and loneliness weren't limited to those with multiple degrees. Abby knew her preoccupation with Robbie to be the cause of her own limited social life. As for Jeremy's, she might have suggested his less-than-warm personality was to blame, if he'd appeared to be looking for answers. He didn't.

"This project is only one of many that I attempt to keep my mind occupied," he continued.

"They're beautiful." She reached out toward the petal of one lushly exotic flower. It grew nearly as tall as she was, with wild green leaves and a blossom like Fourth of July fireworks.

"Watch out for that one," Jeremy cautioned, drawing her back out of reach. "It tends to be a little aggressive."

She stepped back, bumping against Jeremy and catching his cleanly masculine scent among the stronger ones. "Um, how can a plant be aggressive?" she asked, concerned more with his proximity than with the vegetation.

"You don't want to know."

Abby took his word for it, easing away from the plant, and from him. She felt safer already.

"Looks can be deceiving," he explained. "Every plant in this room should not exist. They're hybrids of genetically incompatible species."

"I see," she lied boldly.

He didn't even bother to pretend he believed her. "Plant reproduction is not too different from animals. In nature, there has to be a swapping of fertilization between similar species in order for reproduction to be successful."

"How romantic." Abby forced the inappropriate visual

from her mind. She was certain Jeremy would have been horrified by his starring role.

He gave no outward sign that he had heard her, continuing to describe the love life of plants with cold, scientific precision. There was no hint of the passion she'd witnessed from him in his kiss, no inkling that he had any emotions at all.

"Usually two species must have enough traits in common or they can't procreate," he continued. "That's why there are no cat-dogs running around."

To her surprise, Abby found herself following his explanation. She was certain he could have made the complex topic more complicated or not bothered to explain at all, but his description held none of the ridicule she might have expected from having to lower himself to her standards. She got the sudden realization that he must have been a good teacher.

She risked their fragile truce with a question. "So why are your plants different?"

"They are all combinations of species with genetically different gene pools. Using accepted scientific principals, they shouldn't have been able to mate."

"But these did."

"Sometimes there's no accounting for the mistakes of nature."

She was certain that was true. The fact that Robbie was her son was proof enough.

"However," he continued, "since their genetic makeup is so unusual they will never be able to reproduce. They are too deviant to match with anything else."

"Even another one like themselves?"

"Not even then. These specimens are useful only in their contribution to science. They will only survive in a controlled setting. They can't be transplanted. There is no place for them in the real world.''

"That is so sad." She actually felt a moment's sympathy at the thought that these plants would never have a life beyond this room. It didn't seem right that no one else would be able to experience the beauty of what Jeremy had created. "That must be hard for you after all your work.''

"They're simply the result of experiments," he denied. "I don't have emotional attachments to the byproducts.''

Somehow, Abby didn't believe him. The plants were too well tended, too extraordinary for him not to care, but she couldn't very well call him a liar. She began to make her way back toward the door, the scent suddenly becoming overwhelming. "Well, I appreciate you showing this to me. You seem to have a very interesting hobby here. I wish Robbie could have seen them. I'm sure he'd have been thrilled.''

Jeremy sighed, heavy with frustration. "Don't you understand what I'm telling you?''

Abby turned to face him. "About the plants? Yes, you were very informative actually.''

"Not only the process, about everything.''

He ran his hand through his hair in a gesture of frustration that she'd seen on her husband a hundred times. What was it about her, she wondered, that affected a man's tresses?

"You mean the fact that you consider these plants a metaphor for your life?'' she asked sadly, knowing he believed it. "I got that, too.''

She saw shock as he stared at her openmouthed, and stamped down both the satisfaction that she'd managed to surprise him and the disappointment that it had been necessary. She might not be as smart as he was, but she'd gotten the message. Any connection she thought she'd felt between the two of them had only been a figment of her imagination. They were as different as a cactus and a daisy and there would be no more misguided attempts to link them together. Since she'd known all along about their insurmountable differences, the disappointment she felt came as a shock. Why had she thought he'd be different?

"I realize that, for whatever complex reasons, you and Robbie are unique. I don't have to understand genetics to grasp that. But there's beauty here, too, and strength, and the ability to beat the odds and thrive. Look around if you don't believe me.

"As for the rest of it, I got that message, too. You don't have to worry about me. I'll keep my petals away from your stamen. In the meantime, I have a kid to raise. And a job to do. So I should be getting back to work—unless there's anything else you want to show me?"

"Um, no, I guess that's it," Jeremy muttered, frowning.

Abby slapped her hands together, as if brushing off imaginary dirt. "Fine then. What do you want to do first?"

Chapter Six

"What was your favorite subject in school?"

Jeremy sighed, tired of trying to dodge the never-ending barrage of questions. It was easier, he'd learned, just to answer and get it over with. "Any one that challenged me and taught me something I didn't already know."

"Did you ever have trouble in any of the classes you took?"

He contemplated the myriad of advanced studies he'd been exposed to over the years. "Not that I can recall. Learning new things has always been something that comes easily to me."

He didn't bother to add that this experience with her was perhaps the most perplexing one of his life. True to her word, she'd withdrawn physically—a paradox, since she continued to assail him in every other way. In a routine they'd fallen into during the last few days, she arrived each morning and got right to work, scouring and straightening. After he finally ventured out of his office—the one room he'd declared off-limits to her organizing efforts—she would appear, ready with another round of inquiries.

The questions only added to the torture of having her around each day, close enough to touch, to smell, to watch, but forever out of reach.

Abby passed him a glass of iced tea she'd just finished making. He noticed she avoided any chance contact with him by placing the glass in front of him and moving away. "That's the way it is with Robbie, too. He's like a giant sponge that just wants to keep absorbing and never gets full."

He supposed that was a good enough description of the way he felt, though her own quest for knowledge seemed equally limitless.

He watched her turn to automatically restore order to the space. She didn't like to sit still, he'd found, following her unconsciously sensual movements with his eyes. The constant motion had kept Jeremy in a perpetual state of turmoil.

"Did you ever want to be anything besides a teacher?" she asked, wiping down a counter that was already spotless.

"The first career goal I can remember having is wanting to join the circus and become a clown."

Her hand stilled and she gaped at him openly.

Jeremy was certain the look was mirrored on his own face, the words having escaped from some unknown leak in his psyche. He knew better than to let down his guard around her; she made you say things you didn't want to say, feel things you didn't want to feel.

"Did you say a clown?"

Now that he'd inadvertently let the truth slip, he knew there was no chance that she'd just let it go. "I thought it would be fun to paint your face and make kids laugh,'' he admitted reluctantly. ''Nobody would care how much you knew or what your IQ was.''

He expected her to laugh, but instead she nodded thoughtfully, adding another layer of his soul to her collection.

''What about you?'' he asked, deciding it was time to turn the tables on her. ''Did you ever want to do anything other than take care of people?''

Now it was her turn to look embarrassed. ''I hadn't really given it much thought. Ted didn't like the idea of my having a career. But I remember thinking I'd like to work with little kids, maybe as a teacher, someday.''

Now it was her turn to expect a laugh. He could see it in the way she braced for his reaction. But there was nothing funny about missed opportunities. He should know. ''You'd have been good at it. You're smart, you care about children and you listen.''

Without appearing to think about it, she stuck her leg out at him. ''Sure. Here, pull the other one.''

His gaze locked on the slim, shapely leg. He could imagine running his hand along the soft skin, touching his lips to...

He yanked his attention back, hoping she hadn't witnessed the stark desire he knew had been apparent.

Thankfully she seemed more concerned with his comment. ''You don't have to patronize me.''

He sneered at her, insulted she thought he'd have bothered with false flattery if the circumstances had called for it. ''Haven't you been the one teaching your son, all along? You've been his primary educator up until now, and from what you've said, he seems to be doing okay.''

''That's because of him, not me,'' she denied. ''He

treats learning as a reward and teaches himself most of the time. I have almost nothing to do with it.''

''I disagree. You have no idea the amount of harm that can be done from the wrong influence.'' Unfortunately that was one lesson he'd learned firsthand.

She shook her head. ''I'm just his mother, and I barely manage that job.''

''You underestimate yourself.''

He could see the shock register on her face. It was as if she'd never considered that before. ''That's easy to say for someone who's never failed in his life.''

Was that the impression he'd given her? How far it came from the truth! ''I didn't say I'd never failed,'' he countered. ''My grades have always been perfect, but I saved failure for the really important things.''

''What do you mean?'' she asked.

Jeremy saw the confusion on her face and the way she continued to look to him for answers, answers he didn't have. He couldn't keep the truth from her any longer. She needed to know just how inadequate he'd really been, no matter how painful it would be for him. It would destroy, once and for all, any future involvement between them— which was a good thing, he reminded himself ruthlessly— but it might also help her protect her son from a world that could destroy him.

He started to explain his past to her but the words simply refused to come. How did you describe the ruin of something so valuable, the waste, the regret? Besides, he rationalized, he wasn't even certain she'd believe him. She had a way of seeing what she wanted to see and forging on despite the facts.

He knew there was only one way to get her to see the truth. He would have to show her.

He stood up from the table, the glass of sweetened iced tea suddenly leaving a sour taste in his mouth. "All right. You win. You want to see what it's really like? I'll show you. Let's take a ride."

"To where?" Maybe it was the thought of riding together with him in the car or maybe she wasn't as sure of him as she thought, but she didn't sound too thrilled. It was going to get worse.

"Into town. You wanted to find out what it's like to be me, didn't you?"

"Yes." Though suddenly she didn't sound so sure.

"Then let's go. I'll make sure you find out everything you need to know." Afterward, he was certain she'd have sense enough to run the other way and his life could return to normal.

Quiet, peaceful, alone.

Just the way he liked it. Just the way it had to be.

The car seemed to shrink considerably when they got inside together, causing Abby to understand the true meaning of the word compact.

"Are you sure you don't want to drive?" she asked, still reeling from the fact that he'd walked around to her passenger door rather than insisting they take his car.

"Why bother? Your car is right here."

He honestly didn't seem to have any trouble allowing her that much control. In fact, he didn't even appear to be aware that there was an issue. She'd never met a man who didn't want to be the one behind the wheel—in more ways than one.

She wondered if this was some kind of intellectual test or the greatest evidence of his superior brainpower that she'd witnessed so far.

She put the car in gear and eased out of his driveway, concentrating on the pattern of twists and turns she'd memorized to find her way to the street. The last thing she wanted to do was to get lost, causing her to spend even more time breathing in his masculine scent, feeling her arm brushing up against his every time she turned the wheel. Thinking about what his mouth had felt like against hers.

She reminded herself that the temporary insanity between them was better forgotten, except as an example to keep from repeating. His plant demonstration had made that clear. She just hadn't expected the lesson to be so hard. Abby wondered if she was forever doomed to make the same mistakes, finding herself attracted to a man she had nothing in common with.

He was right, of course. She had to concentrate on what was important—Robbie's welfare—rather than picturing the way Jeremy's eyes had softened up close or the way she imagined his desire to have an edge of desperation to it, as if he was drowning and she was a life jacket.

With that goal in mind, she decided to use this opportunity of forced confinement to bring up a situation with Robbie that had been niggling in the back of her mind. And if it helped keep her mind off Jeremy's nearness, so much the better.

"I dropped Robbie off at camp this morning," she began, unsure of where to start, unsure even of what was bothering her.

"Hmmp."

"He says he really likes it there. There's so much to do."

"Good for him."

"They've got arts and crafts and swimming. It's just

like you said—he needs to be treated just like a normal boy."

For the first time since they'd entered the car together, he turned in her direction. "But he's not a normal boy."

It figured. He was correcting her already. "I understand that—better than anyone. But you said it's important for him to have fun."

"What's fun for the other kids might not be fun for Robbie."

As they neared the center of town, a car pulled out from a side street and Abby braked to give it room. "What do you mean? He says he's having a great time."

"Hmmp," he responded again.

Did Jeremy know something she didn't know? The absurdity of that question almost made her laugh. "Don't hmmp me! Tell me what you think."

He sighed, obviously reluctant to explain, maybe because he didn't think she'd understand, but she had no intention of giving him a choice. However, before she could figure out how she intended to force him to talk, he began to elaborate.

"It's just that someone with Robbie's abilities might get bored with activities faster than so-called normal children. He needs to be stimulated, challenged. If you ask a kid like Robbie to spend his time coloring inside the lines and playing hopscotch, he's liable to go crazy."

Something about his own words seemed to cause a flash of pain to cross his face, but Abby was too distressed by her concerns for her son to question it. She began to think about his reaction to camp in a new light. She'd sensed something was off, she realized now, but had she been ignoring the signals he'd been trying to send? "Someone who's bored with arts and crafts might, say, recreate the great pyramid out of macaroni? Not to scale, of course.''

''Exactly. But the important thing would be the reaction he received. Was he complimented for his imagination or criticized for not following directions in stringing the macaroni together to make an ugly necklace?''

Abby didn't know what the reaction of his leader or group had been. She hadn't asked. ''But what about friends?'' She thought of the two boys she'd seen with him when she dropped him off each day. ''Doesn't he need to find people his own age that he can relate to?''

Jeremy turned toward her, his arm brushing against hers. He jumped back as if shocked with an electrical spark and his eyes flashed to hers before he looked away quickly. ''Finding someone who can relate to him may be difficult,'' he said, sounding pained. ''It will be nearly impossible to find someone he has anything in common with.''

She knew he spoke from experience, although the warning seemed to indicate the present as well as the past. ''Why is it so hard? Why can't people just get along?''

She glanced over, waiting for the face she'd seen on her ex-husband a thousand times—the one that said she was naive and foolish. Instead he began to explain.

''If you were in first grade, learning the alphabet and struggling with addition, and the kid next to you was working on quantum physics, would you want to be their friend?''

''Maybe.'' Now she saw a familiar look on his face— one that said he doubted her. But rather than try to convince him, Abby countered with a question of her own. ''What about the smart kid? Would he want to hang around with the slow one?''

''It depends on the kid. It might be his greatest wish.''

She realized the conversation had gotten personal somehow. "But you're saying a relationship wouldn't last, aren't you?" she asked, hearing the opinion in his voice. "Because they'd have nothing in common?"

"The odds would be against it."

Odds he could probably compute to the nth degree. Odds, he'd determined, that left no room for them despite what she thought she'd felt between them.

On top of her mistake about Jeremy, she was afraid she might have also messed up with Robbie. Again! Abby was beginning to accept the almost constant feeling of being overwhelmed but she'd been so certain she was finally making the right choices for her son. It was no wonder nobody ever listened to her opinion. She was always wrong.

This time it was Abby who opted for silence, finishing the rest of the drive trying to stamp down the sudden need to end this trip—whatever Jeremy's secretive reasons— and go to Robbie. She barely registered their arrival in town, with its ornate Victorian houses and blooming flower boxes, as she pulled up in front of the quaint general store and parked.

Jeremy didn't rush to fill the void with false reassurances. Because she didn't expect him to, it was a surprise when he spoke.

"One thing I've learned is that there is no right answer for every person. Perhaps I'm wrong and Robbie is having the time of his life. Or maybe all he needs are a few in-depth projects to keep him interested. Talk to the camp. Talk to Robbie. You're a good mother. You'll figure out what to do."

This time it was her turn to *"hmmp."*

Together, in the quiet confines of the car, Jeremy placed

his hand over hers. Although she knew he only meant to comfort, her heart beat faster.

"Don't listen to me." His sullen growl contrasted with the tenderness of his touch. "I sometimes respond to things in a negative way."

Under different circumstances, the understatement might have made her smile.

"It's one of the side effects of seeing so many things that other people miss. It's impossible to ignore all the unfairness in the world. It's one of the reasons I stay by myself. So nobody has to put up with my gloominess."

It was only the second time since she'd met him that Jeremy had attempted to soothe rather than antagonize— and the explosive results of the first time were still fresh in her mind. It occurred to her that she should have been grateful for his gruffness; his tenderness was irresistible.

"Don't worry," Jeremy continued. "Robbie has everything going for him. He's smart, he's strong. And he's got you. I'd say he's a lucky boy."

Something about the way he was looking at her made the words clog in Abby's throat. "Do you really think so?"

"Do I seem like the kind of man who would lie just to protect your feelings?"

She'd never doubted that before. Yet she hesitated before responding. "I suppose not."

"Then why don't you wait and see what happens? I've found there's no reason to borrow trouble. It usually finds you soon enough."

She knew he'd developed that pessimistic attitude the hard way but Abby had another view. "And if the worst happens, you work as hard as you can to make the best out of it."

"Are you sure it's safe to be walking around with your head in the clouds that way?" She could have sworn she caught a hint of teasing in his tone.

"As long as I don't come crashing to earth," Abby responded, enjoying the verbal word play.

The game ended as his eyes became serious again. "I wish you didn't have to."

Jeremy forced himself to pull his gaze away from the perfection of her face. No matter what Abby thought or hoped, there was no way to keep her from crashing to earth—at least as far as he was concerned. What would it have been like, he wondered, if things had been different and he had more to offer than an abnormal mind and a scarred life?

As his vivid imagination created an array of possibilities to taunt him, Jeremy noticed the town's pharmacist limping along the sidewalk, leaning heavily on his cane. The older man's gait slowed as he noticed Jeremy inside the car and peered through the windshield with a curiosity that bordered on rude. Because Abby was fumbling with her purse, he knew she hadn't noticed.

Just as he knew that the moment they stepped out of this car together, his chances to pretend there was some hope for them would end.

For her sake, he opened the door.

"Let's get this over with."

He didn't have to look to see that the smile had faded. Or that her shining eyes would have lost a little of their glow, the way they did when something dented that heart she kept pinned on her sleeve as a target. He shouldn't be thinking that he'd like to yank her into his arms instead, to kiss her until those eyes smoldered with another kind of light, the kind he'd seen before. He shouldn't be tempted to do a whole lot more than that no matter who was watching.

He could just imagine the town's reaction to that!

But he couldn't do that to her, any more than he could allow her to continue to believe that he was just some smart and lonely guy who could help her figure out her son.

He got out of the car before he could change his mind. She followed him silently, glancing down the street to where the pharmacist had stopped a crony to gawk. Unaware of the reason for their scrutiny, she simply smiled at the two older men. As Jeremy watched, they both straightened. He could have sworn that the paper-white skin of one of the men took on a rosy blush as they smiled back with invigorated masculine interest.

My God, her effect was universal. It was no wonder he felt captivated.

They entered the general store together. There was a larger, more modern chain on the outside of town, but this one did a good job of stocking the staples while managing to appear old-fashioned and charming. And, like the general store of yesterday, it served as the gossip center for the town. He knew they'd find more than milk and bread here.

They were barely inside before he heard the first whispers. "Look who it is…"

"Did you hear what happened to…"

"Never the same…"

He looked at Abby to gauge her reaction but she seemed oblivious. "What do you need?" she asked him. "I assume you're all set with soap?"

It took him a minute to understand the reference. "I don't need anything."

"Then why did we come here?"

Jeremy would have liked to tell her and get it over with but he knew she'd find out soon enough. "I felt like getting out."

She nodded, without questioning the lie. She had no way of knowing this would be the last place he'd voluntarily return to. "I might as well stock up on some cleaning supplies while we're here," she said. "There's still a lot of work to do at your house."

Work, he was sure, he'd be handling by himself after today. "That's fine," he responded indifferently.

As she began to walk on ahead, unsuspecting of what would come next, Jeremy held back, putting some distance between them. Now that he was here, he found himself reluctant to go through with his plan. Once she saw how people treated him—and why—she would never look at him the same.

He told himself it was for the best. She should find out now before they got any more deeply involved. Although, when he thought about returning to his normal life after she was gone, he feared she might have already done irreparable harm.

He heard several people call out her name in greeting. She had only been in town for a few weeks, yet she had already been accepted to a degree Jeremy had never found. He knew the cause to be his own fault, and soon she would, too.

Abby rounded the corner of one of the aisles, nearly colliding with one of the locals Jeremy recognized. The man had been part of the crowd that had gathered outside the general store all those years ago. When he saw the way the man looked at her, Jeremy felt a flash of some strange emotion that almost felt like... Jealousy? No, it couldn't be. The violent, possessive urge to punch the guy must have some other cause.

He just wished he could come up with one, Jeremy thought as he stepped out from behind the end shelf.

"There you are." Abby glanced up and smiled when she saw him. "I thought you'd gotten lost."

"The store is set up in a fairly simple grid pattern," he replied. "I managed to find my way without any difficulty."

The man's eyes widened. "You know Dr. Waters?"

"I'm working for him."

"But didn't I hear that your son is some kind of genius? I'm surprised that you would…"

"That I would what?"

Tell her! Jeremy urged mentally, knowing the time had come. Tell her about the night Leonard had gone on his rampage. About the car the twelve-year-old had stolen from another, older student. About the accident, maybe self-directed, nearly fatal, in front of the General Store. About the public breakdown and the ambulance that had taken him away. About the sudden, silent withdrawal of students he was supposed to have been helping instead of destroying.

Tell her, he thought, before I have to.

"It's just that— Nothing. Never mind."

"Okay," she agreed without hesitation, walking away without seeming to give his warning a second thought. She had crossed to another aisle before Jeremy could register the reprieve.

As she tossed assorted items into her basket, Jeremy couldn't help but relive that awful night and the many others that had come since. After the breakdown, Leonard had spent years in an institution and had never regained a normal life. He'd tried to stay in touch but Leonard's parents had asked him not to come back anymore. He didn't blame them.

He would never get over the potential of that brilliant child wasted because of him. Jeremy had been so sure of himself, so cocky about his abilities. Although he'd been aware that the incidents of emotional problems were higher in people with extraordinary abilities, he must have underestimated the problem. He might have even caused it with his assertions that he could find a way to make them fit in.

He'd been wrong. Someone like him would never fit in.

Abby picked up a bottle of furniture polish, but rather than looking at the bottle, she stared at him with concern. "What do you think of this one?" Her voice was purposely cheerful. "It's lemony fresh!"

He controlled the urge to slam it to the floor. "It doesn't matter."

She put it back on the shelf and picked up another. "You'd prefer the pine scent?"

Exasperated, Jeremy snatched another bottle from the shelf and shoved it into her hand. "Don't you want to know what that man was talking about?"

She examined the label carefully, as if the choice of product were of the greatest importance. "Not especially." She turned the bottle over. "This looks good. I've never seen this brand before."

He sighed. "It's made completely with products found in nature and it's safe for the environment."

"How do you know?" She looked at the label featuring a stream running through a line of towering pines. "You know, this looks like a spot I pass on the way to your house. Did you make this?"

Jeremy frowned, momentarily distracted. "It's put out by Naturally Yours, a small company specializing in organic products."

"But it's yours?" she pushed. "You created it? Brewed it up in that kitchen of yours?"

Jeremy couldn't believe she'd guessed. "I might have worked on the solution, but the company was started by one of my former students. He was concerned about all the chemicals they put in cleaning products and wanted to do something to help the environment. I helped him find the right combination of ingredients."

At the end of the aisle, a mother pushing a baby carriage began to approach, saw him and backed up, crashing into the end display in the process. Abby looked up in time to see her retreat around the corner.

"And the soap?"

"It was a test batch for a new recipe he's trying," he admitted.

"You must be very proud."

Actually he couldn't remember thinking much about it before now, but he realized it had been rewarding to watch one of his students grow and thrive. Until she'd mentioned it, however, it hadn't occurred to him how gratifying that success had been to him personally.

Unfortunately one success didn't make up for his other terrible failure.

"It's a good thing nobody else in town has figured it out," he said as another customer poked his head around the corner to stare. "They probably wouldn't stock it if they knew."

"Why? Is it a bad product?"

"No, it's a great product."

"Well then, that would be just stupid, wouldn't it?"

Jeremy didn't have a response to that. He had no defense for the foolishness of holding one person's actions against someone else.

It occurred to him that the same sentiment could apply to his connection to Leonard, but he pushed it away. Now she had him doing it! he thought in frustration. But he hadn't been just an innocent bystander. He had been responsible for that breakdown and for the child himself.

The town certainly hadn't forgotten. Even if he wanted them to.

Yet Abby seemed oblivious to the clues.

Just as he was beginning to consider explaining everything himself and getting it over with, he saw a familiar face headed toward them and knew he wouldn't have to.

"Good morning, Mrs. Crawley," Abby greeted her dour landlady. The Sunshine Lodge had not earned its name through any connection to the disposition of its owner.

Mrs. Crawley didn't even respond to the greeting, instead turning her scowl in his direction. "What are you doing here?" she challenged.

Abby answered for him, looking pointedly in the direction of her cart. "We're shopping."

"I meant with him!" She glared at Jeremy as if the force of her stare would be enough to wither him. It almost succeeded.

"He's shopping, too," Abby replied calmly.

"Didn't you understand what I told you before?" Mrs. Crawley demanded, her shrill voice rising even higher. "Don't you listen to reason?"

"Not according to my ex-husband," Abby acknowledged bitterly.

Suddenly this whole idea of bringing her into town to let them break the news to her seemed like a bad one. It made him feel cowardly and guarded. And worse, the feeling wasn't unfamiliar. It reminded him uncomfortably of the last few years of his life.

Jeremy tried to intervene, even knowing it was too late. "Mrs. Crawley, I assure you—"

She ignored him. "I warned you." The woman shook a pointed finger in her direction.

Nonchalantly, Abby began to nudge the carriage toward the front of the store. She had to squeeze through the crowd that had begun to gather.

Mrs. Crawley followed, throwing visual daggers at him behind her back. "This man is dangerous. Do you know what he's capable of?"

"I couldn't begin to imagine." Somehow, she made the assertion into a compliment, as she began to pile the bottles of furniture polish and assorted items onto the counter in front of a wide-eyed cashier.

At that moment, Jeremy would have traded fifty IQ points to get them both out of that store before disaster struck, but short of dragging her out—which he was certain she'd fight on principle—he had no choice but to wait as another scene of his life played out on center stage.

Mrs. Crawley made one more attempt to get through to her. "He's done things. He's not normal, I tell you!"

She turned toward Mrs. Crawley with a cool calm that seemed the opposite of what Jeremy was feeling. "Being normal seems to be the one thing I haven't heard him accused of. But when did that become a crime? Because my own son is obviously guilty of the same offense."

Jeremy had never had anyone defend him before. It was a unique experience—even if she was wrong.

Abby looked around her at the rapt faces of the strangers watching her shopping expedition. "What's the matter with you people? Haven't you ever seen a supergenius before?''

There were a few gasps, followed by a thick silence, which was broken rather startlingly by the shrill of some-one's cell phone. It took Abby a few seconds to realize the sound came from her purse, opened on the counter. ''Who would be calling me?'' she asked, fumbling for the phone. ''Nobody has this number except... Hello?''

She listened for a moment before responding. ''I understand. I'll be right there.'' She turned to Jeremy, all thoughts of her audience forgotten. ''It's the camp. There's been some kind of problem. They want me to come get Robbie.''

Her purchases forgotten, he took her arm and they rushed from the store together.

Jeremy wasn't sure whether or not she heard Mrs. Crawley as she called out behind them. ''Ask him about the other boy. Ask him!''

Chapter Seven

Robbie! Something had happened to Robbie, Abby thought numbly as she left the store. They'd told her he hadn't been hurt but she couldn't imagine what else could have happened. Maybe they were just waiting for her to get there before giving her the bad news.

Fighting against a rising panic, she realized Jeremy had followed her outside. The tiny rational part of her brain that was still functioning knew he'd just faced some kind of gauntlet inside. She didn't want to abandon him but she couldn't think beyond getting to her son.

"I'm sorry," she said. "I've got to get Robbie. Can I drop you somewhere?"

"Let's go. I'll drive," he said in response, holding out his hand for her keys. "I know a shortcut."

She passed him the keys, for once grateful to have someone else to rely on, if only for a little while. She wasn't sure she could have made the trip alone.

This drive was made in silence and took too long, despite the way Jeremy navigated quickly through the narrow side streets. When they reached the camp, he ignored the signs for parking and drove straight up to the front door. She didn't stop to thank him before rushing inside, though for some reason it was reassuring to know he'd be nearby.

She saw Robbie the moment she entered Drew's office. He was sitting in a chair in the corner, looking healthy and undamaged. She breathed fully for the first time since her phone had rung.

Gradually she became aware that Drew and Robbie weren't the only ones in attendance. There was the pony-tailed counselor and the boy who'd punched Robbie in the arm, along with a woman who looked like an older version of the pug-nosed, brawny little boy in a dress.

She felt as if she'd just walked into an ambush.

"What's going on here? Is Robbie all right?" She looked to her son for confirmation, but he seemed to be avoiding her gaze.

"Your son is fine," Drew responded, rising from his desk. "As is everyone else, luckily."

Everyone else didn't look fine, she thought. The counselor's face was flushed as was the mother's. The little boy was the only one who appeared happy to be there, making faces at her that the others couldn't see.

"I'm afraid we've had an incident here," Drew said. "It seems that during nature time, Robbie got somewhat carried away with his knotting techniques."

"He tied me up!" the little boy cried out. "Now he's gonna get in trouble!"

"I don't understand," Abby said.

"It appears that while Sarah was showing the children how to make a few simple knots, Robbie fastened Kevin's hands behind his back and tied him to his chair."

"I don't know what he did but I couldn't get him free,"

the counselor responded. "All the kids were laughing. We finally had to cut him free."

Robbie spoke for the first time. "It was a simple Bowline knot. They kept making it worse."

"Your little boy is a menace," the mother yelled. "He doesn't belong here."

Abby looked at Robbie, who went back to studying the ground. "I don't know what to say." It was just like Jeremy had warned. He hadn't fit in here at all and she'd been kidding herself. How could she have been so wrong?

"I'm afraid we can't allow that kind of behavior here at this camp," Drew responded.

She saw a twinge of regret in his face until the mother looked in his direction. Then he hardened his expression into a stern scowl.

"I don't understand. He's never done anything like this before," she floundered. She wanted to protect her son but she didn't know how. He wasn't making any effort to defend himself or offer an explanation. She was at a loss as to what she could do.

To her surprise, she heard Jeremy speak from behind her. She hadn't realized he had followed her in or that he'd been listening. After this morning, she couldn't imagine why he'd chosen to put himself in the line of fire again. Or why she suddenly felt so much better.

"I happened to notice that the only boy Robbie decided to restrain is so much bigger than him." He leaned against the door, eyes narrowed and arms folded across his chest, as if he'd just happened by and discovered someone who could help him solve a tricky riddle. "If he'd been inclined to cause trouble, why didn't he pick one of the other, smaller children? That seems like it would have been a wiser course of action for such a smart kid."

Every eye in the room flashed toward him with various

degrees of hostility. Like a lightning rod during a bad storm, he took a direct hit.

"What is it to you?"

"You've got a nerve, sticking your nose in."

"This is none of your business, Waters. He isn't one of your students—thank goodness."

Abby looked at Robbie, huddled in the corner, continuing to clutch his arms around himself and rubbing his shoulder. The same spot she'd seen Kevin punch this morning in what she had thought of as a friendly gesture. Now she wasn't so sure.

"He's got a point," she said, trying to think. As the collective glare returned to her, Abby spared a thought that if Jeremy faced this kind of disapproval on a regular basis, it was no wonder he'd decided to keep to himself. "Can you think of anything that might have caused Robbie to act out like this? He's never had behavior problems before."

The counselor shrugged and avoided her gaze. "I dunno."

"Was there any reason Robbie might have wanted to pick on this particular child?" she asked. "Any problems between them before? Or was this a random act?"

The girl blushed to the roots of her hair. "They've had a few fights before. Kids are always messing around like that."

"Did Robbie start the fights?"

"Um, I dunno." Her eyes flashed to Kevin's mother.

"It's a simple question, really," Abby said without accusation. As usual nobody seemed to notice anything deeper than her pleasant exterior. "Who would you say was responsible for starting the fights?"

"Um, probably Kevin might have started them."

"And did Robbie say anything to you before today?"

"I told Mr. Danforth," the young girl blurted. "I told him Kevin's been picking on him. He wouldn't leave Robbie alone."

Abby realized what had been happening, and what she'd been missing all along. She turned to Drew. "I spoke to you this morning." And just about every other morning since she'd arrived. He'd pursued her relentlessly, yet never bothered to mention anything about the trouble her son was having at the camp. "Why didn't you say anything about this then?"

"This kind of thing happens—"

"When you allow it to happen," she finished. She walked over to her son and held out her hand. "You were right. This type of behavior can't be allowed. Robbie obviously doesn't belong here."

She noted that everyone in the room looked startled except for Jeremy as she took her son and left.

The only question was what she was going to do now.

"Can I speak to you in private for a minute?" Jeremy asked when they'd arrived back at his house.

Abby looked into the back seat where Robbie had put on a headset to listen to Spanish language tapes. Her motherly instincts were still working well enough to know her son was also trying to avoid the discussion he knew was coming. But he wouldn't be able to stall for much longer. A serious conversation between them was long overdue.

In the meantime, she thought with a sigh, she might as well deal with one problem at a time. She knew what Jeremy wanted to talk to her about. Since Robbie was obviously not returning to camp, he was going to tell her she couldn't come back. He hadn't been vague about his conditions. He didn't want to be directly involved with her son. She'd known all along that it had been a temporary arrangement but she hadn't expected to feel this sense of loss that threatened to overwhelm her.

"I'll be right back," she told Robbie before getting out of the car.

Jeremy's face was unreadable as he waited for her outside. "Can you come inside for a minute? I have something to give you."

"Sure." She kept a smile pasted on her face, determined to end things on a positive note.

As she followed him into the house, she wondered what he had to give her. If this had been a normal arrangement she might have expected a final payment with her discharge, but this had been anything but a normal arrangement.

He paused in the hallway just inside his door so that she could still see the car. Abby took a deep breath, determined to get this out before he shooed her away. "Thank you for your help today."

"I didn't do anything."

She smiled sadly. "For such a smart guy, you're not a very good liar."

He shrugged. "I thought there might have been more to the situation than they were disclosing."

"I guess that's a problem you've dealt with before? People hassling you for no good reason? For the record, I think they're off base. You're not the scary guy they think you are."

"Yes, I am." His voice was low and pained and somehow intimate in the small room.

"No, you're not. If you were, you wouldn't have kept trying to scare me away."

"What kind of logic is that?" Jeremy asked.

"My kind."

How could he fight against reasoning like that? Jeremy

thought as he found himself smiling at her. He realized the expression didn't feel as foreign as it had a few days ago, the result of too much time spent in her proximity. She was like a beacon: constant, bright, hopeful. Not only her looks, which although stunning, paled in comparison to the person inside. Just being around her made a person want to believe that everything might work out.

Damn it. He hadn't ever wanted to feel that way again.

With an effort, he turned the silly grin into a scowl as he picked up several pages of paper from the table and handed them to her.

She frowned at the list he'd compiled. "What is this?"

"It's a list of schools and programs you might want to look into for the fall. All of them have extensive experience with gifted children."

"Just like that?" she said, scanning the sheets. "I've been searching for weeks and I didn't come up with any of these names."

"These are mostly small, private programs. Because there are so few children who need them, the information's not readily available to the average person."

She looked up, meeting his eyes, and he realized how that might have sounded. Calling Abby average was a little like calling himself somewhat bright, but now that the words were out, trying to take them back would only make matters worse.

"I appreciate this," she said. "I didn't expect you to go to all this effort for me."

"It was nothing." He cringed again at his choice of words but this time she didn't react.

"It is to me." Her bottom lip quivered with emotion.

His gaze locked on her full, pink mouth with a hunger that was almost frightening. The coil of desire that had taken up permanent residence in his stomach since the day he'd met her reared and struck. He was surprised the force of it didn't hurl him across the room, or worse, draw him nearer to close the meager space that separated them.

Then she made a move to bridge the gap by holding out her hand with an offered handshake. He had no choice but to take it, the softness of her palm against his further torment.

"Thank you," she said. "For everything."

He kept hold of her hand, barely registering the finality of her words. With one small tug she would be in his arms, his mouth on hers, her chest crushed up against his as he sated himself or tried to. Yet only their hands continued to touch, the semblance of a handshake disappearing with every passing moment.

Jeremy realized he should say something, but the synapses of his brain seemed to be misfiring. "I'm acquainted with most of the schools on that list," he managed finally. "I wouldn't have recommended them if they weren't good, but take a look and see what you think. They all have strengths and weaknesses that should be considered before you decide. I'd be happy to answer any questions you have about their programs."

She nodded the way people do when they think you're making an offer for the sake of being polite. This close, however, he could see her eyes cloud with sadness. He wondered at the cause. He'd expected her to be pleased, not disappointed.

When she withdrew her hand from his and stepped back, he felt bereft. It shouldn't have been such an unusual sensation.

Taking the hint, he retreated to the other side of the table. It wasn't enough of a distance—he wasn't sure there was enough distance in this hemisphere—but at least he could think clearly again. "So, what are your immediate plans?" he asked her.

She shrugged, avoiding his eyes. "Like you suggested, I'll take a look at this list, then maybe Robbie and I will hit the road to see a few of them."

"You're leaving?" It was the first time the thought had occurred to him. She would go and he would never see her again.

"I thought… You said…" She paused and took a deep breath. "I didn't think you'd want me to come back. I'll have to keep Robbie with me. I'm not sending him back to that camp and I don't know anyone around here well enough to ask them to watch him."

He hadn't considered that, hadn't considered his plan at all for that matter. That fact, along with a feeling close to panic, caused him to snap his response. "That hasn't changed. I don't want anything to do with him. If you want to come back, I'll keep working with you, but you'll have to keep him away from me. There are lots of things around here to keep him out of the way."

For the first time since she'd barged into his life, Jeremy saw a real chill come over her. The difference was startling, turning sunshine to ice. He wanted to take back his words, but he couldn't. He couldn't take a chance of getting close to Robbie. For the boy's sake.

"I would have thought that you, of all people, would have been different."

"I am. That's the problem."

She nodded with acceptance, even as her disappointment raked over him. "I'll have to think it over," she said. "I appreciate what you've done but I have to consider Robbie first."

She looked him in the eye and he saw his failure reflected there.

"If I decide to come back," she said finally, "you can tell me what happened to the other little boy."

When Jeremy opened his door to them the following Monday, Abby thought she caught a flicker of relief. It was followed by a quickly masked flash of pain as he looked down at Robbie.

Despite the intense self-debate that had prompted her decision to return, Abby almost took her son and ran in the opposite direction. He shouldn't have to deal with another person in his life who didn't want anything to do with him. He'd already faced that kind of abandonment when his father left. Although he'd been very young at the time, his amazing brain allowed him to understand things other children couldn't comprehend.

No matter what her reasons for returning, she wouldn't have taken the chance of bringing Robbie around if she thought Jeremy would hurt him in any way. As far as she could tell, it was the only good part of the restrictions he had insisted on. Jeremy couldn't disappoint him as long as they kept their distance.

Unfortunately the same couldn't be said for her.

"Melrose & Company, reporting for duty." She ruffled her son's curls before remembering he didn't like that.

He didn't seem to notice, though, as he was staring intently up at Jeremy. "Did you really win the Mathematics Institute Award when you were only ten?" Robbie asked with awe.

"I did." Jeremy's curt response seemed to be dragged from him.

"I'm going to enter that someday."

"You should."

Abby knew Robbie had begun to develop some kind of hero worship since Jeremy had accompanied her to the camp. Since role models for someone with her son's mind were scarce, she hated to discourage his interest, though she wished he'd chosen someone who wasn't afraid to look at him.

Hoping her son didn't notice the abrupt answers, she interrupted the conversation. "We have a lot to do today. If we're going to get it all done, we should get started."

Robbie seemed to realize he was gawking—which even for a five-year-old wasn't cool. "I promised my mother I wouldn't touch anything." He controlled his enthusiasm with a restraint beyond his age.

"There's nothing you can hurt. Except for my private office, you can go anywhere in the house—as long as your mother is with you."

And as long as he didn't go near Jeremy, Abby added mentally, grateful, at least, that he hadn't pointed out his conditions to her son.

"Why don't you go get your bag out of the car, honey?" she urged. With all the activities she'd brought to keep him busy, he wouldn't have the chance to get in Jeremy's way.

As Robbie darted back to the car, anxious to get inside, Abby turned back toward Jeremy and felt the automatic one-two punch of desire and disappointment. Now that they were alone, his face was set in a grim mask that reminded her of the first time she had seen him. But it couldn't erase the sensuality that she now knew ran deep. She'd been a married woman, she'd had a child, but she'd never known the yearning she'd felt when he'd taken her hand as if to hold her close instead of letting her go.

She ignored the feelings, knowing they didn't change the facts.

"I didn't think you'd be back," Jeremy said, surprising her with his bluntness.

"I'm not sure I'm staying."

"But you're here now. Why?"

"I don't like to leave a job unfinished. I still have work to do on the dining room, the kitchen…"

He wasn't buying it. "Why did you come back here?"

Abby should have known better than to try to fool him, but she wasn't sure she had an answer to his question.

It might have been more sensible to put as much distance as possible between them and Jeremy, but she'd decided she needed more. Her plan had been to find out how it felt to be a genius, what it meant and how to help ease the way. But what she'd discovered only led to more questions.

What had wounded him so deeply that the scars had never healed? Why had he closed Still Waters and what had happened to the little boy? How could she keep the same thing from happening to Robbie? His experience with the camp had made her realize she was still a long way from understanding how it felt, just as her experience with Jeremy made her realize she must have been wrong when she'd thought she'd seen something hidden beneath the gruff exterior.

If there was any other reason for her return, she refused to consider it.

"I realized I still had a lot to learn. No surprise there, I suppose—"

"Why do you do that?" he interrupted, his voice sharp. "Put yourself down? Since I met you, I haven't seen any indication that you're anything but astute and intuitive."

She didn't know how to respond to that. Nobody had ever described her that way. "Not smart enough, apparently. I thought I understood…certain things." About Robbie. And about Jeremy. "I was wrong." About everything.

"If I'm going to protect him, I've got to know what I'm up against."

"Are you planning to protect him against me?"

"If necessary."

He nodded, satisfied. "Then we shouldn't have any problems."

Robbie raced back across the lawn and into the house without any hint of the concern Abby was feeling. "Is it all right if I look around?" he asked. "To acquaint myself with the surroundings?"

Jeremy didn't answer directly, but she noticed a slight nod of his head giving permission.

"Sure. But be careful." The standard mother's warning was more from habit than concern. She didn't intend to let him out of her sight.

Like a normal five-year-old, Robbie dashed into the house, eager to explore. He barely paused in the living room she had worked on, though Abby noted Jeremy had kept the depressing curtains open. As Robbie poked his head into some of the rooms, she followed at a distance with Jeremy by her side. Even standing next to him was enough to keep her nerves tingling with awareness. Although they were both careful not to touch, it was as if he had some kind of magnetic field around him, pulling her closer. Maybe he'd invented some kind of attraction device. Or maybe there was a simpler explanation. Abby had fallen in...lust with a man who didn't want anything to do with her son.

Robbie stopped suddenly in one of the doorways. "You've got your own game room," he said in awe. It wasn't the mindless arcade full of pinball and violent simulations another boy might have appreciated. Instead tables were set up with chess sets and games she couldn't begin to figure out. One wall held a bookcase filled with puzzles and brain teasers. It didn't take much to imagine Jeremy's students gathered here to challenge each other and themselves.

"Go ahead and look around," Jeremy told him, speaking to him for the first time without being asked a direct question.

Robbie didn't need to be told twice. He ran into the room and began to wander, pulling out boxes to examine the contents and moving a piece on the chess board after a few moments of consideration. Jeremy might not have wanted him around, but at least he didn't seem to mind the disturbance.

Knowing her son would be kept busy at least for a while, she took the opportunity to step outside the room. It had been a difficult decision to return but there were a few things they needed to settle between them before she decided whether or not to stay.

"I need to know what happened to the other little boy. Will you tell me?" They both knew it was a test.

"Leonard," Jeremy responded, for once not attempting to evade. "His name is Leonard."

Abby noticed he hadn't used the past tense. It was a small detail, but it helped put her mind at ease.

A pause grew until Abby began to think he wasn't going to answer. Finally he began to speak, his voice filled with such pain she almost begged him to stop. But she had a feeling this was something they both needed to get out in the open.

"As you've discovered, people don't always accept those they don't understand."

Abby thought about Robbie's experience at the camp as well as hers in trying to understand what went on in Jeremy's mind. But there was no need in pointing out the obvious.

Jeremy sighed. "I had an idea that I could create a place where kids wouldn't feel so left out, where everyone would understand each other. Where they wouldn't have to feel like they were always on display, always the outsider."

He kept his voice low, so it wouldn't carry to Robbie. "At first everything was great. The combination of personalities and ideas allowed us to share our thoughts. We pushed each other while still offering support. We had some great discussions and brainstorming sessions. Everyone could be themselves and not worry that others would think they were strange if they chose to listen to Mozart instead of rock and roll."

Abby could see his pride and thought it must have been great to be a part of that environment.

"The kids looked to me for guidance," he continued. "They trusted me, looked up to me. Like Robbie did a few minutes ago. Yes, I saw the expression on his face. How would you feel, as his mother, if I took that hope and destroyed it?"

She tried to imagine Jeremy purposely hurting her son and failed. "I don't—"

He didn't wait for her to finish, appearing to be caught up in his own memories. "We were kind of a self-sufficient community so they didn't need many opportunities to go into town. Maybe that added to the isolation or maybe we just felt so superior that we thought we didn't need anyone else."

"That's not your fault," she pointed out.

"It *was* my fault. If I hadn't raised their hopes so high, they wouldn't have fallen so far."

"So your crime was giving hope?"

"Nothing so noble. That last night, one of my students, a boy named Leonard, proved once and for all that my grand plan was nothing more than a pipe dream. He'd been having trouble, experiencing symptoms of depression, feeling overwhelmed. I saw the signs and tried to help. He was seeing a doctor. But it was too much. He snapped. Went on a rampage through the town, destroying cars and property. He almost killed a little girl.''

She could tell the prospect still haunted him. ''There was nothing you could do.'' Somehow, she was sure of it.

''He was my responsibility. It was my fault. Afterward, the rumors about what had happened spread through the town and fed on themselves for fuel. The stories got ugly and crazy. Most of the students' parents pulled them from the school. After a while, the others left on their own.''

Abby could only imagine what that had done to him. The school had been his dream. ''What did you do?''

''What could I do? There was nothing to be said or done.''

''You didn't explain? Defend yourself?'' Even as she asked the question, she knew the answer. Jeremy wouldn't have defended himself, not because he didn't think they deserved an explanation but because he thought he deserved the blame. It was no wonder the town looked at him as something of a freak. He'd given them no reason to think differently.

Abby felt the anger that had carried her through the last few days begin to disappear, to be replaced with a keen sense of loss, for Jeremy, his students, and for herself.

It seemed perfectly natural for her to cross the distance between them and to place her arms around him the way she might have if Robbie had been hurting. He froze at her first contact, but then drew her closer. With her head against his chest, she heard his heart start to race. She'd intended only comfort for someone who was suffering, but the tingling that began to spread through her body was anything but comforting.

She felt the whisper-soft touch of his lips on top of her head and knew he hadn't meant for her to notice. It was the single most seductive experience she'd ever had in her life. She had only to raise her face to his and the situation would change. Instead she eased away, not trusting herself to make the right decision. That wasn't what he needed right now.

He cleared his throat and tried to hide the desire in his eyes. He failed. "That wasn't the reaction I was expecting."

"You keep surprising me, too." She wondered if he'd ever stop. In that instant she made the decision about coming back. "If it's still all right, I've decided to keep working with you."

"I don't want your pity."

"Is that what you think I'm feeling?" She wished it were that simple.

"This doesn't change anything. I won't take the chance of getting close to another special child. There is nothing I can do to protect him."

Abby pictured Jeremy's struggle to figure out what was happening to his student. She knew he'd have used everything at his disposal to help. Yet he'd failed anyway.

"If you couldn't manage it," she asked, "what chance do I have alone?"

Chapter Eight

Jeremy could hardly notice yet another presence in his home.

Except for the hum of chatter that filled the once comfortable silence, the occasional bursts of laughter, the footsteps clattering through hollow halls, the scent of her perfume noticeable even above the lemon-scented cleaner, the music, the singing, the crayon under the table, and the feeling of being a prisoner in his own home.

Other than that, he barely knew they were around.

It had been a week since Jeremy had told her about Leonard and gotten her surprising reaction. He'd expected horror, but got only compassion. He'd expected her to push him away, but instead she'd pulled him close. He didn't know what to expect anymore.

She worked her way through his house like a whirlwind, banishing dust bunnies and replacing order when he hadn't known it was missing. And she'd kept her promise to keep Robbie away from him, approaching Jeremy with questions only when her son was busily occupied with one of the multitude of projects she arranged for him each day.

So why did he feel like punching a hole through the bedroom wall?

Rather than dwell on that particular question, he decided to pursue another, more intellectual one. He'd been meaning to get to work on finding a way to grow roses without thorns. So what if it had little scientific significance. At least it would keep him out of her way.

Creeping down the back staircase like an intruder in his own house, he made his way toward the library where he had a book on horticulture.

He'd barely made it through the door when he saw he wasn't alone.

Robbie looked as startled to see him as he was to run into Robbie. He was struck again by how young the boy was, how childlike despite his advanced abilities. Physically he didn't have anything in common with Leonard, whose tall, gangly body had added to his sense of awkwardness. There was no reason for Jeremy's palms to have become suddenly damp or his heart to thud as if he were fleeing danger.

Robbie stared at him, directly and unblinking. His eyes, so similar to Abby's, added another layer of regret.

"My mother says I'm not supposed to bother you."

"You're not bothering me," he lied.

The fact that he accepted Jeremy's answer without question proved how vulnerable he was. "I told her you wouldn't mind. I'm looking for a book on space exploration." He picked up a book and showed Jeremy the cover.

"That's a good one," Jeremy managed to say. It had been one of his favorites as a child, full of pictures and diagrams, though he didn't share that information.

"I'm going to be an astronaut when I grow up. I'm going to explore Mars."

"Your mother told me. That will be interesting." It didn't occur to Jeremy that his response had assumed future success when most people would have treated the comment like a child's whimsy.

"Some people don't believe me."

He shouldn't be giving advice but he couldn't let the opportunity pass. "Don't let other people tell you what you can and can't do."

There was that look again. That look of...faith. It struck Jeremy like a dagger, making him think about the losses of past—and the future. "I've got to get going. Help yourself to anything you want in here."

"My mother is interested in you."

Robbie's words stopped Jeremy in his tracks. Had she said that? After much practice he'd begun to think of their encounters as flukes, brought about as a result of his neglected sexual drive and Abby's affectionate nature. Anything else between them was hopeless. As hopeless as Jeremy being able to ignore Robbie's comment.

"She is?"

Robbie nodded. "That's why she decided to come back here."

"Oh, um..." He'd known there had to be some reason she'd chosen to ignore his warning and return. He just hadn't presumed that her reasons were personal.

"She's interested to find out how I'm going to turn out when I grow up."

Jeremy's ego did a quick crash and burn. Of course she was only interested in him as a test subject. He'd known that from the beginning. There was no reason to be annoyed just because his interest in her had become so much more complicated.

"She says it has nothing to do with chemistry."

"Chemistry?"

"Yeah. My mom told me it's just chemistry that's making her confused. She was talking about you and trying to decide what to do, talking out loud like she does sometimes to figure things out. She said that the problem is just chemistry and that it's not important." His voice dropped to a confidential whisper. "My mom's not very good at chemistry."

Jeremy wouldn't say that. She'd certainly created her share of combustible reactions around him.

"Are you interested in her, too?" Robbie asked.

He gulped, out of practice answering tough questions. He knew it wasn't unusual for young prodigies to cross boundaries others might consider impolite. It was their nature to question everything. "In what way?" he hedged.

"About what she likes and doesn't like, things like that. Because I can tell you all about her, if you want."

It was a tempting offer. "I don't think I'll need any help in that regard. Your mother and I are just..." What?

Luckily he didn't have to figure out an answer to that question when Abby walked through the door to the library.

"There you are. I told you that you could get a book and come right back." She glanced with concern between Jeremy and her son.

Jeremy knew she'd be a lot more worried if she'd overheard the direction of their conversation.

"I'm sorry if he was bothering you. I told him you shouldn't be disturbed."

"He wasn't bothering me," he lied a second time. Although actually, he'd been more disturbed than he cared to admit to discover she'd been thinking about him.

She placed her arm around Robbie's shoulder protectively. "I explained that you have an important project that you've been working on."

She was making excuses for him, he realized, to cover for his absence. He hadn't given much thought to how Robbie would view his avoidance. It just went to show how thoughtless he could be.

"That's true. And I should be getting back to work," he responded, hoping she'd recognize his silent appreciation. With one final glance at the way they stood together as one, he left the room.

"Bye, Jeremy!" he heard the cheery farewell.

Abby looked down at her son with suspicion in her eyes. "What are you up to, young man? I've seen that look on your face before. The time you set the kitchen on fire trying to test the fire extinguisher."

"There was no damage done," he pointed out. "And besides, I'm not doing anything." His expression was innocent, angelic.

Now Abby was really worried. "I know you think Dr. Waters is great—" and she'd found herself unable to smudge that image no matter how much his continuing attitude had hurt her "—but I don't want you to get your hopes up too high." It saddened her to realize it was the first time since he'd been born that she'd had to tell him that.

"Don't worry, Mom. I won't."

She wondered why she wasn't convinced.

Having finished the major jobs of scrubbing and polishing, Abby was now concentrating on the smaller, more detailed work. Robbie had been helping her dust all morning which meant she'd only had twice as much work to do. But the result of spending time with her son had been worth it.

Abby liked cleaning. She knew it wasn't the most prestigious job and that many people looked down on someone who would pick up after others for a living, but she enjoyed putting things in order, making things shine.

However, no matter how much she worked on Jeremy's house, she couldn't find the sense of satisfaction that usually came from setting things right.

Maybe the trouble was that there was no one around to mess it up.

The house needed people, to live in it, to learn in it, to bring light to a dreariness she couldn't shine. Until it had that, she was only fixing the surface.

She understood Jeremy's concerns about letting down Leonard and his other students, but she couldn't agree with his conclusions. Would he have been so upset if he was half the villain he considered himself to be?

Certainly Robbie didn't think so. He'd been singing Jeremy's praises almost constantly since he'd run into him in the library. She only hoped Jeremy didn't do anything to destroy that admiration.

Speak of the devil...

Tingles ran along Abby's spine, telling her she was no longer alone. She should have figured he'd show up since she'd just given Robbie permission to go outside to play. It had become a ritual of sorts for Jeremy to just happen to show up when Robbie was occupied elsewhere.

The habit was getting on her nerves. The kid didn't have cooties, after all. Maybe it was time to remind him of that fact. If he couldn't deal with that then perhaps they'd be better off to leave him alone as he obviously desired.

She turned to find him standing in the doorway, halfway in as if he wasn't sure he wanted to get too close. Abby stamped down the automatic jolt she got in her stomach when she saw him. She was sure there was a scientific explanation for it, just as she was sure she probably wouldn't be able to understand it if someone explained it to her.

"Have you got a minute?" he asked.

"Sure. This is a good time, actually. I'd like to talk to you about something."

"I want to talk to you, too. Before Robbie comes back in."

"That's just it. I..."

He stepped into the room carrying a long white telescope that was nearly as tall as he was with its expandable silver legs. "I wanted to give you this. For Robbie. It's a telescope."

"I can see that." Even if she hadn't recognized it from one of the upstairs bedrooms where it had been pointed permanently towards the stars, she'd have remembered it from reading Jeremy's book. He'd bought it himself when he was just a boy, using money he'd received from his first published article.

He leaned it with care against the wall. "I was thinking about his interest in space and thought he might like it."

"Like it?" He'd flip. It wasn't one of those kiddie models that were sold in stores. This was the real deal, probably capable of looking into the eyes of the man in the moon. "I don't know what to say."

"It's no big deal. It's not like anyone's using it anymore."

Abby didn't buy that. Not for a minute. She had the strongest urge to cross the kitchen and wrap her arms around his neck. She just wasn't sure the reaction was due to his offer. She also didn't think the gesture would be appreciated, judging by the way he stayed on his side of the room, as if allowing him an escape if necessary.

"He can keep it," Jeremy added. "You can take it with you when you go."

The fact that he'd dropped their leaving into the conversation with such ease took a little joy out of the moment but she refused to be distracted.

"That's very generous of you but—"

"It's nothing. You can give it to him when he comes in."

It wasn't nothing, although she could tell he wasn't comfortable with the gesture even as he made it. "Why don't you give it to him yourself?"

"I've got more important things to do than to be giving presents to some kid." His voice took on that dangerous sneer she recalled from their first few meetings, but unfortunately for him, the tactic no longer worked.

"But that's what you just did, isn't it?" she replied reasonably. "Give Robbie a gift?"

"Don't read more into it than there is." His raised voice made the scowl more fierce.

"You'd hate that, wouldn't you? If someone got the idea that you cared? If you growled and grumbled and nobody got scared?"

The description didn't actually apply to her. She was scared, all right, but she wasn't ready yet to admit the reason.

Now Jeremy was the one who looked afraid. "I don't know what you're talking about."

"You're so smart. You figure it out."

The back door slammed before he could respond. "Mom!" Robbie's voice rose over the rumble of running feet. "I found a great bug. Come look."

When she turned back, Jeremy was gone.

Robbie's shrieks of excitement had sent Jeremy into hiding for the next couple of days, but finally he could no longer stand being a prisoner in his own home. Or so he told himself until he approached the kitchen and heard them chatting.

"Did you know that the human body needs sunshine to produce vitamin D?" Robbie asked.

"I didn't know that," Abby answered distractedly.

"And did you know that according to my weather station, there is an eighty-five percent chance of rain tomorrow?"

"That's great, honey," she answered. "But we are not going outside until I finish this."

Robbie sighed with melodrama that only a five-year-old can manage, but despite the dramatics, Abby wasn't swayed.

Jeremy gave her credit for her parenting skills. She gave Robbie a lot of attention, but she didn't tolerate tantrums or tricks and didn't allow him to outsmart her to get his own way. Which, come to think of it, was pretty much how she'd dealt with him. He didn't know whether to be impressed or insulted.

She explained herself to her son with a calm, reasonable tone. "I told you that I have to organize these cabinets before we take a break. Do one of the puzzle books I brought for you."

"I already did them all."

"All of them?"

"Yup. They were easy."

Jeremy took a deep breath and prepared to enter the kitchen. He'd presented papers to scientists and debated icons. He could face one little boy and his bothersome mother.

He walked into the room and found her in the process of emptying his cabinets and sorting the items by category on top of his counter. As she moved efficiently through the mundane task, he couldn't help but watch the flow of her arms, the twist of her body. Jeremy had never realized cleaning could be so seductive, but then, everything about Abby was seductive.

He banished those thoughts from his mind, a mental exercise that had begun to occupy his time like the attempt to decipher an unsolvable riddle.

When Robbie noticed him, his pose changed from leaning on one elbow, staring into space, to upright attention. Jeremy recognized the admiration and awe on the boy's face and felt worse.

"Jeremy!" Robbie called out.

At the sound of his name, Abby swung around, her expression even more unsettling than her son's. He saw welcome and pleasure to see him, the warmth in her eyes spreading across her face and transforming it to something beyond beautiful.

"Looks like you're making progress," he said for lack of anything intelligible to say.

"I am," she agreed. "I'm almost done with this section of the kitchen and then we're planning to go outside to have a picnic. Would you like to join us?"

"No." Because the answer was abrupt to the point of rudeness, he tacked on, "Thank you."

"I understand. You're still working on your special project," she said for Robbie's sake, but he could see the disappointment that now shadowed her features.

Jeremy wished he actually had some project to keep him busy. Maybe then he wouldn't keep thinking about Abby. Before she arrived, his days had been filled with a variety of solitary activities, physical labor and mental projects. Anything to keep his mind occupied. Lately, however, there didn't seem to be anything in particular that needed to be done.

Like Robbie, he found himself restless and bored. He supposed the same would have been true for any young boy facing forced confinement, no matter what his IQ.

"If you'd like," he offered to Abby, "I could finish that up for you and you could head out now."

Abby looked down at the towers of cans and boxes overflowing his countertop. "I don't mind. I'm almost finished."

He could hear Robbie's muffled groan.

"You know, it's not necessary for you to keep cleaning around here. I told you I'd help you anyway." It was a conversation they'd had several times, but he tried again. He'd already promised to help her narrow down the list of schools he'd given her, figuring out which ones best suited Robbie's needs. It wasn't necessary for her to continue working at menial labor.

Her chin tipped up in a gesture he was beginning to recognize. "We have a deal. I'll hold up my end of the bargain."

Jeremy's sigh echoed Robbie's earlier frustration. She got insulted when he suggested she didn't have to clean his house and clung to him when he confessed his part in a tragedy. What kind of woman was he dealing with? He was beginning to think he'd never figure her out.

He knew it was hard for her to juggle taking care of Robbie, working for him and finding time for the work they were doing together. But he also knew it must be hard for Robbie—not that the boy's welfare was any of his concern. He had no intention of getting involved.

Although, he supposed it wouldn't hurt to give him something to keep him busy.

"You know, there are some ingredients right here in this

kitchen that could be used to create some experiments. Completely safe, of course. Do you think it would be all right if I show Robbie how to make some chemical reactions?''

Robbie began to bob in his chair. "Can I, Mom? Can I?''

"Chemical reactions? Are you sure it's safe?''

Jeremy nodded, realizing he was trapped now that he'd made the offer. He wondered why he didn't feel the panic he'd expected. "It's kid stuff, really. He might not even be interested.''

"I am. I am. *Pleeease,* Mom.''

"I guess it would be okay,'' Abby agreed with a smile that could melt a block of ice. Afraid it already had, he turned toward a jubilant Robbie, who looked like a five-year-old who'd been promised an amusement park instead of chemistry.

"Let's see if we can make something happen,'' he suggested.

Abby couldn't erase the smile from her face as she looked over at the two goggle-covered faces. Jeremy had tried to remain aloof at first, showing Robbie what to do and then stepping back to let him handle everything alone, but he'd slowly been drawn in by her son's technical questions.

She'd been prepared to step in if she heard Jeremy snap at him like the ogre he seemed to think he was or belittle him as her husband used to do. Instead she watched them babble on about atmospheric conditions and thermodynamics and saw the way Jeremy patiently answered his questions and prompted him to delve deeper.

Although she was glad to see them establish a rapport, she knew it wasn't going to have much of a chance to grow. The time was nearing when she knew she'd have to leave. When that time came, she had a feeling they'd all miss something. Robbie: someone who understood him. Jeremy: the chance to share his knowledge. And Abby. She was afraid to put her feelings into words, but she thought she might lose the most of all.

They leaned closer to get a look at something, Robbie's light curls against Jeremy's dark hair. Her son's almost angelic looks and Jeremy's hard and haunted. They couldn't have looked more different, yet they had made a connection she never would. She wished she could have been the one to answer all her son's questions, to help him with his studies, to ask questions that made him think instead of ones he had to explain to her.

Jeremy had no problems with the complex challenges. She was struck again by how extraordinary he really was. She'd known it all along, of course, but listening to him as he allowed free reign on his thoughts with her son, she wondered why she'd been kidding herself with thoughts of a relationship between them. There were sparks, sure. He hadn't been able to hide them, no matter how he tried. But, as Jeremy had just explained to her son, you needed more than sparks to keep a fire going.

"Mom, come look at this."

Since she'd finished organizing the kitchen cabinets, there was nothing to keep her away, but she was hesitant to join the activities.

"I was going to put our picnic together," she answered. "If you'd like, we can go outside now."

He didn't even look up. "Not now, Mom. We're adding the final ingredient, liquid nitrogen. This is going to be great."

The plan had been to experiment with things Jeremy had around the house, and Abby was still dealing with the fact that he'd happened to have some liquid nitrogen hanging around. According to Jeremy, they were making ice cream, though she'd believe it when she saw it.

"Maybe your mom would like to help us," Jeremy suggested.

Robbie looked shocked at the very idea. "She doesn't like this kind of stuff."

"Too tough for her? Or do you think she just doesn't want to get her hands messy?"

Rather than the real disdain she might have expected for someone as science-challenged as herself, she heard the dare in Jeremy's comments. "I can do it, if you two can." Without dwelling on the ridiculousness of that comment, she joined them at the counter.

"She'll have to put on protective gear," Jeremy cautioned. "Safety first, right?"

"Right," Robbie agreed, while continuing to stare at her as if afraid she'd lost her mind.

Jeremy took off his goggles and handed them to her, then dropped an apron over her head. The glasses were too big, even when she tried to adjust them, so Jeremy helped secure the strap, her nape tingling where he touched. After pulling on the rubber gloves he required, she turned around.

Robbie's jaw dropped comically as he gaped at her before dissolving in a fit of laughter. Jeremy made an effort to keep a straight face but it was too much of a struggle. His deep, husky laughter sounded rusty as it joined her son's high-pitched giggles.

Recalling how Jeremy had looked in a similar getup while making soap, she could imagine how she looked. But for someone whose primary focus had once been her looks, the embarrassment of appearing silly was nothing compared to the joy of listening to the laughter that filled the kitchen. She preened and strutted like a runway model, making fun of herself for their enjoyment.

Robbie howled with laughter, delighting in the spectacle, but slowly, Jeremy's laughter ceased and he began to look at her as if she was wearing a sexy negligee instead of an oversize apron and rubber gloves. Abby was used to people looking at her. She'd learned to ignore it, knowing they only saw the shell. But there was something about the way Jeremy looked at her, the desire, the heat, the admiration, that made her feel beautiful inside and out.

Robbie seemed to notice the change in the atmosphere. Though she was sure he didn't understand the sudden tension, his laughter slowed and he looked back and forth between them. Abby moved closer, not wanting him to get the wrong idea, as she took her place in front of the bowl they'd placed in the sink.

Jeremy moved in behind her. Although their bodies weren't touching, she could feel his breath on her neck, the sensation incredibly erotic. Abby struggled to concentrate as he explained the process, but his words slipped by unheeded. It had been so long since she'd been intimate with someone, felt the strength of a man's body next to hers, smelled the masculine scent that she was inhaling now.

She shouldn't be thinking like this with her son next to her, she knew, but with Jeremy so close it was hard to control her thoughts. By the time he was ready to add the final ingredient, she feared she might explode herself.

Jeremy lifted a silver container and began to pour the contents into the bowl of cream and sugar.

The first cloud of sizzling steam had her grabbing Robbie to rush to the safety of the other side of the kitchen.

"It's okay, Abby," Jeremy hurriedly explained. "Perfectly safe, I promise you. I told you it would react that way due to the change in temperature.''

Abby's heart was thudding loudly in her ears, her eyes wide, as Jeremy calmly mixed the steaming ingredients. ''I knew that.''

''I told you she wasn't a science person,'' Robbie announced, his giggles returning.

She stepped closer, nervously looking into the bowl and saw with surprise that the liquid was already turning into something resembling her favorite dessert. Even more hesitantly, she looked to Jeremy, wondering what his reaction would be to her blunder. She already knew how her husband would have reacted. But instead of criticism and embarrassment, she saw only understanding and acceptance.

Why had she ever feared this man? Abby wondered, more shocked by the question than she'd been by the steaming chemical. Why would anyone? Clearly Jeremy was incapable of hurting anyone. She'd been right about him when she'd accused him of hiding. He was the one who'd been hurt, so badly that he'd retreated behind a mask, afraid to be hurt again. That didn't make him a beast. As far as Abby was concerned, that made him a kind and gentle man who'd lost the thing he cared about most.

''Now comes the best part,'' Jeremy told them. ''We get to test the results of our experiment.''

''Yippee,'' Robbie responded.

''Yippee,'' Abby echoed faintly.

Chapter Nine

Somehow, it made perfect sense to bring the ice cream to their picnic. He told himself his agreement to join them wasn't related in the least to the fact that standing so close to Abby, inhaling her scent and imagining her strutting around his kitchen in *just* the apron and gloves, he hadn't been thinking with his brain. It was also irrelevant that he'd begun to want Abby so badly that spending time with her had become a penance of its own, one that would surely have made up for his past multitude of sins, if he'd been inclined to request forgiveness.

He wasn't. And nothing had changed. He was just going on a damn picnic.

Abby spread the blanket out in a patch of sunshine at the edge of his property, placing the cooler she'd brought as a picnic basket in the middle. Robbie claimed his spot by sprawling along one whole side and Abby took the other corner leaving the last quarter for Jeremy. As he sat, wondering what to do with his legs to keep them from tangling with hers, he realized he'd never been on a picnic before.

They ate the ice cream first, to Robbie's delight, and concluded that the results had been satisfactory. He tried not to be insulted that Abby seemed so surprised by their success. Then she opened the cooler and passed out the sandwiches in little plastic bags, fruit drinks and cookies that appeared homemade. The sandwiches, he found, were peanut butter and jelly cut into little fun shapes. Another first, he thought, as he took a bite and discovered the taste of the common household staple. He couldn't have been more delighted if she'd brought along strawberries dipped in chocolate with a bottle of champagne.

"You like peanut butter and jelly?" she asked when he chose another, one of the star-shaped ones this time.

"I do. It's good."

"I'm glad you like it. It's Robbie's favorite."

Jeremy took a sip of the syrupy fruit drink, but found it too sweet for his liking, although he figured it would suit a five-year-old's taste perfectly. He tried to picture his parents providing him with this kind of meal when he'd been five, and failed.

"My mom's a good cook, but she's not much of a scientist," Robbie said with a giggle.

He could have sworn he saw something flash across Abby's face. Disappointment? Embarrassment? But it was quickly hidden, as she leaned across the blanket to respond to the comment with a tickle. "Well, it's a good thing we already have one scientist in the family then, isn't it?"

Robbie wriggled frantically, trying to escape her prodding fingers but his mother was crafty and found the spots that sent him into hysterics.

Jeremy leaned back, watching them together. He'd had many aspirations and ideas through the years, most of them cerebral in nature. Yet, it suddenly occurred to him that somewhere along the line, he'd missed a few valuable lessons.

How would it feel, he wondered, to be a part of this setting: a man, a desirable woman, a terrific child? He tried to picture it, but failed to imagine the scene with anyone but this woman, this child.

And that option was not a possibility.

"What's the matter?" Abby asked, noticing his sudden stillness. "Are you feeling all right?"

"Everything is fine." Or if it wasn't there was nothing he could do about it. "I just ate too fast."

"I always have to remind Robbie to chew his food. You two can be pretty dumb for a couple of smart guys."

"I suppose you're right," he responded, taking her comment seriously. Although he'd never realized the extent of his foolishness before.

"Hey, look," Robbie said, pointing up at the sky. "It's the moon."

They looked into the sunlit sky to see a barely visible reflection of an almost full moon. "That's called a Buck Moon," Jeremy explained.

"Really?" Abby said. "I didn't know that."

"I'm a fountain of useless knowledge." Apparently it was only the important stuff that he'd missed along the way.

Robbie jumped up from the blanket, suddenly too excited to sit. "You know what we should do? We should take your telescope out tomorrow night and look at the moon."

"Robbie!" Abby scolded. "I'm sure Jeremy has better things to do than to spend his time amusing us."

Actually, at the moment, he couldn't think of a thing. "It's okay. I don't mind."

She stared at him. "Are you sure?"

He didn't want her to make too much of his agreement. "It's not an imposition. Staring into space happens to be one of my favorite things to do."

"Mine, too," Robbie chimed in.

"That's funny. I like it, too," Abby admitted. "I used to spend a lot of time on the roof of our old apartment, looking out at the night sky."

Jeremy wondered if she'd been looking for something, or trying to get away from something. He thought he knew the answer. Abby didn't run. It was a trait he admired, although he knew, even if she didn't, that there were some fights you couldn't win. He hoped it was a lesson she never had to learn.

At his agreement, Robbie began to run around, skipping in the tall grass and whooping with joy. Jeremy couldn't remember the last time he'd been able to bring that much happiness to one person. There had once been a time when the sound of laughter and excitement had been common in his world but that had been a long time ago.

Abby began to collect the remainder of their lunch. "Thanks for being so nice to Robbie today." Her voice was soft so it wouldn't carry. "You were good with him."

"He's an easy kid to like." His lowered voice matched hers and somehow left him with the feeling of being secluded and intimate despite the fact that they were still sitting out in the open. "Anybody would have done the same."

A shadow passed over her face. "That's where you're wrong. It's not easy for some people."

"Some people are fools."

She glanced at him with gratitude. "I get so scared sometimes that he'll never find anyone to really understand him."

"You? Scared?"

"Constantly."

He'd have thought nothing ever bothered her. She seemed to face every obstacle—including him—fearlessly. Knowing she experienced anxiety like everyone else but then faced those fears to do what needed to be done gave him another layer of respect for her.

"What are you afraid of?" He knew it was a personal question, way over the limits of the relationship they'd established between them but he couldn't help himself.

She didn't answer right away and he wouldn't have been surprised if she ignored him but instead she seemed to give it careful thought before responding. "My biggest—my only—concern is for Robbie. He's everything to me."

As if on cue, they both looked over to where he was busy adding to the dandelion population by picking the flowers that had gone by and blowing the seeds into the wind.

"I'm afraid of not measuring up," she said softly, almost to herself. "Of not being good enough."

He knew exactly how she felt. Those concerns had once been his most terrifying worries. He didn't tell her how much more devastating they could be when your own failures brought those fears to pass. He pushed the memories aside, knowing from experience that agonizing over what he could have done differently wouldn't help.

"Look what happened today," she said as an example. "I got involved and ruined your experiment."

"You didn't ruin it," he answered with a smile. "You made it more interesting." Much more interesting, from his point of view.

"I should have left you two alone. You were doing so well together."

"Robbie loved it when you joined us."

"He's five years old. He doesn't know any better."

"I'm twenty-nine. What's my excuse?"

Her gaze jumped up from the ground to meet with his, and Jeremy realized he'd revealed too much. "It's always more interesting to add an unexpected element to any experiment."

"That's just a fancy way of saying I messed things up. If I can't handle ice cream, how am I supposed to handle acid and a Bunsen burner?"

"Very carefully?" he suggested dryly. When his joke didn't bring even a hint of a smile, he continued. "You're serious about this, aren't you?" He knew she thought of herself as lacking in education, but he hadn't seen anything other than solid thinking and a wisdom that went far deeper than any school book.

"I'm sorry I brought it up. I don't want to talk about it." She started to rise, but Jeremy held her in place. This was too important.

"You don't think I'm going to let you off that easily, do you? After the way you've analyzed my life for the last few weeks, I'm afraid you're just going to have to deal with a little examination of your own."

Abby winced, silently admitting defeat.

"You know, don't you, that you have more common sense and logic than anyone I've ever met." It was something she needed to be told, something she should have been told a long time ago.

"Common sense? That's nothing."

"It's nothing to you because it comes naturally, just like calculus does for me. Which do you think is more useful?"

She shrugged.

"You don't have to understand everything Robbie knows to understand Robbie. You're there for him, you support him, you push him to be a better person, yet you allow him to be himself. What more could he want?'' What more could *anyone* want? "There's more to intelligence than what's in books.''

"That's easy for you to say.''

"It isn't. Believe me.'' It was the hardest thing he'd had to learn and she'd been the one to teach it to him. "You know people, not things. That's an amazing gift.''

She finally stopped trying to avoid his gaze and looked at him. Although he knew it was a mistake, he let her see everything he was feeling, everything he'd been afraid to feel.

"You're smart. How can you doubt it? You've been outsmarting me from the day you got here.''

"Well, that wasn't that difficult, really,'' she joked.

"And you've got a great sense of humor. It will help you deal with whatever's ahead.''

The smile faded as she seemed to realize he was serious. "I think I'm going to need it.''

"And you're caring. I've never met anyone with more capacity to feel. I only worry that you care too much.''

She shook her head. "That's not possible.''

"And stubborn. Let's not forget that. You're very, very stubborn. I'm sure that trait is going to take you far. You can achieve whatever you want.''

"I...''

Apparently she'd been rendered speechless. It was a first.

There was one trait he hadn't mentioned, one she could have no doubt of. She was sexy, incredibly, wonderfully sexy. Although he'd tried to stamp down those feelings, he knew she could tell what he was thinking by the way her eyes widened. Despite the fact that Robbie was only steps away, or maybe because of it, Jeremy allowed her to see the depth of the hunger he felt for her. For some reason, after all she'd learned about him, it was important that she understood that—even though he knew it would change nothing.

"What about the future?" she asked cautiously. "About a school for Robbie?"

"What about it?" he asked, not surprised that she'd still be putting Robbie's needs first. It was one of the traits he admired most about her.

"I still haven't figured out what we're going to do." She looked at him expectantly, as if hoping he could provide the answer. But it wasn't that easy. There were still many variables to consider.

"You'll figure it out. I have faith in you. Just ask yourself what you want."

"I know what *I* want," she assured him.

"And Robbie? What do you want for him?"

"The same as for everyone else, I suppose, understanding, acceptance, respect."

He couldn't have said it better himself. "What about location? Does that matter?"

"I suppose that isn't an issue," she said slowly. "Unless you can think of any reason why it would matter." Inexplicably she stared at him for a long moment.

He shrugged, sure it was his own imagination that made him see more into her comment. "It's up to you."

She lowered her eyes, nodding. "Then I guess it's not important. We're going to have to move no matter what we do, so where we end up isn't as important as finding the right place."

The thought of her moving halfway across the country brought a lump to his stomach that didn't sit well with the heaviness of the peanut butter, but there was nothing he could say.

She turned away, her gaze following Robbie as he now

collected a bouquet of fresh dandelions. "It would be nice if I could find someplace where there's lots of room," she said. "A country setting like this, where he can think."

"Okay. Good. You're narrowing it down."

"The most important thing is that I want to be involved. Not that I can teach him that much, but I still want to be a part of his life."

"You're the biggest person in his life, Abby. He'll learn the important things from you."

He thought he might have seen tears in her eyes but couldn't be sure.

Abby took a deep breath and let it out in a whoosh. "What about your school? Why don't you teach him?"

Jeremy jolted as if she'd struck him. "What? I'm not opening the school again! I can't. I won't! And I'm not going to teach Robbie, either. How could you ask me to after what I've told you?"

"What happened with Leonard is not your fault," she insisted. "He was troubled. You said so yourself. You were trying to get him help."

"That's not the point."

"I think it's exactly the point. You couldn't have stopped what happened."

Jeremy jumped up from the blanket, startling Robbie as he approached with his gift of crushed flowers for his mother.

"I am never going to open Still Waters again. Never!"

He stalked away, leaving them both staring after him with identical troubled expressions.

Jeremy had told her she was smart and he was right. It was time she started acting like it.

There was no chance for a future between them. She didn't know when she'd begun to think about sticking around to have Jeremy help her with Robbie, but he'd made himself very clear on the possibilities of that happening. He had no intention of asking them to stay.

She had no choice but to start seriously looking into those schools. The summer was more than half over. Instead of prolonging their time here, wondering what might have happened if things had been different, she should be planning to visit the most likely candidates while there was still time.

He walked into the study just as she finished talking to one of the prospective schools. They'd been very interested in talking to Robbie, even more so when she'd mentioned Jeremy's name.

He looked tired, she thought, defeated. Because of her.

She wished she could take back her suggestion but she knew they would both be better off in the long run with her having made it.

"I hope you don't mind me making a few calls," she said. "I finished earlier than I'd expected and you weren't around for me to ask what else you'd like me to do." In fact, she was running out of work in general. Except for his guarded office which she still hadn't seen, the house glistened. It was getting harder and harder to think of things to keep her coming back.

"I don't care if you use the damn phone."

That was the problem in a nutshell, she thought. He didn't care. She refused to let it matter. "I just spoke with someone from the Braitman University. Or Brainiac U as it's nicknamed. They want me and Robbie to take a ride down there to visit someday."

"That's a good idea," he said distractedly.

It wasn't exactly a sobbing plea to stay, but what had she expected? "I haven't said anything to Robbie about it yet. I've barely seen him today. He's been busy researching constellations so he can impress you. He's so excited about tonight.''

"That's what I wanted to talk to you about.''

"About tonight? Is there a problem? Robbie told me the forecast calls for clear skies.''

"The problem isn't the weather. I'm just not sure it's a good idea for me to go along with you two.''

"You're not going?'' She couldn't believe it. Robbie was going to be devastated. He'd been looking forward to this all day. How could Jeremy disappoint them—Robbie, she amended—like this? Despite his gruff behavior, he'd never let her down before. She'd begun to believe she could count on him.

He looked pained. "I'm trying to do what I think is best.''

It was an unfortunate choice of words. Her ex-husband always said the same thing, shielding himself by being reasonable and rational—and somehow always reaching the conclusions that suited him the best. She rose from behind the desk and circled it to stand in front, inches separating them.

"How could your not going possibly be the best thing for Robbie?''

"I don't want him to get the wrong idea.''

She thought of yesterday and the fact that she'd done just that, but he wasn't going to take out her mistakes on her son. "The wrong idea about what?'' she asked.

"About me. It would be a mistake for him to get too attached.''

"That would be a tragedy, wouldn't it?'' Even through her disappointment, she saw what he was trying to do. He'd had fun the day before. They all had. But because of her suggestion, he was trying to retreat back inside that crusty shell of his. She wouldn't allow it.

"Still Waters is closed for good," he insisted. "I am never going to open it again."

"I believe you made yourself clear on that point yesterday."

"I gave it a try and it didn't work out. I won't make the same mistake again."

She wondered who he was trying to convince. Her or himself? "I don't blame you," she agreed. "Especially if that's the advice you used to give the kids. 'If you try once and fail, you should never try again.' It's not a very motivational message."

His face contorted into something dangerous looking. "Don't try to twist this around. It's not going to work. You're right. I wasn't good at it. Not good enough."

That's not what she saw when she watched him with Robbie, but she couldn't convince him of that if he didn't want to listen. "That's your decision. My concern is Robbie."

"That's who I'm thinking about, too. I don't want him hurt." She could see his own agony, even as he made the admission. His voice dropped to a near whisper. "And I don't want you to be hurt."

It sounded as if he actually cared. It was too late to keep her from being wounded by his attitude, but she could still protect Robbie. "He's going to be hurt if you cancel. And he's been hurt enough."

"That's not what I'm trying to do."

"I know." Despite everything, she believed him. "But you made a promise and you should keep it." She took a deep breath and let it escape. "After tonight, if you want us to leave, we'll go. Robbie will never have to know why."

Jeremy stepped back as if he'd been slapped. "I don't want you to leave," he said, sounding shocked.

Abby's heart lurched, not sure she had heard correctly. She'd have asked him to repeat it if she wasn't sure he'd take it back. "What *do* you want?"

"I…I don't know."

It wasn't the response she was looking for.

"I only wanted to protect him."

"Why don't you leave that up to me? Nobody is going to hurt my son. Not you. Not anybody. I won't let them." No matter what it cost her.

"I wasn't trying to insinuate that you wouldn't."

Maybe not purposely, but it had hurt just the same.

"I'm just not sure what you want from me," Jeremy admitted.

Abby wondered what his reaction would be if she told him. "Why don't we try being friends and see how that works?"

"Friends?"

The way he said the word almost made her offer him a dictionary so he could look it up. "You know, people who share their problems and help each other out? No pressure, no expectations. We can just keep each other company until it's time for us to go."

"Friends. I think I can handle that."

"Good. Well then, I guess I'll see you tonight."

She watched him walk from the room, their new pact barely settled. She could foresee only one problem in the agreement.

Maybe Abby should have mentioned that she'd fallen in love with him.

Chapter Ten

The full buck moon rose in the sky, appearing majestic and romantic even for those who knew it was little more than a giant lunar rock. The night had turned clear and bright, bringing comfortable relief from the scorching temperatures of the day and causing the stars to actually appear to twinkle.

Jeremy supposed it would have been too much to hope for a few rumbling thunderclouds. Perhaps it would have dampened the fairy-tale feel of the night.

As they settled back on blankets, not far from where they'd had their picnic the day before, he could smell the scent of Abby's shampoo, clean and sweet, above the candles he'd placed around them. The chirp and hum of distant night dwellers served as background music for Robbie's nonstop chattering.

"Is this a good place to set up the telescope? Do you think we'll be able to see Venus? How many constellations are there all together?"

"Yes. Yes. And too many to name," Jeremy answered the questions in order.

He looked over to where Abby was settling onto the blanket. She'd traded her usual overalls for a pair of shorts and a plain white T-shirt. He attempted not to drool as she leaned back on her elbows and peered up at the night sky.

What had he been thinking when he'd accepted her offer of friendship? He didn't know the first thing about the kind of relationship she had suggested—although he was fairly certain it didn't entail some of the ideas that were currently running through his mind.

He'd only known he didn't want her to go. He was still reeling from the shock.

He saw Robbie struggling with the weight of the telescope and went to help. "Pull the legs out to help support it," he instructed, watching as Robbie intently followed his directions.

As soon as it was set up, the boy rushed to look through, pointing the end toward the sky.

"Wow!" It was all he could manage and a hushed silence filled the night for the first time since they had arrived.

Jeremy's eyes met Abby's with a connection that didn't need words. Witnessing the stunned awe on Robbie's face, the unspoken dreams, the wonder of infinite possibilities, they smiled at each other and enjoyed the moment.

Did friends often share this kind of wordless communication? he wondered. Having never had anyone close enough to fill that role, he couldn't be sure, but it seemed logical. Maybe this friendship thing wouldn't be so bad after all.

The quiet didn't last for long. Soon Robbie began another round of rapid-fire questions which Jeremy attempted to answer or to encourage Robbie to figure out himself.

My God, he'd missed this. He hadn't realized how much. Feeding a child's hunger for knowledge, watching the excitement that came from raising as many questions as he solved. The thrill of witnessing a young mind expand.

And Abby knew it. Looking over at her as he brainstormed the problem astronomers faced with light pollution, he saw her sad smile and realized she'd known it all along. Not that it changed things. She obviously understood that as well.

Maybe that's what being friends was all about—understanding each other. If so, he had a long way to go, because he still had no idea why she'd want to establish a deeper bond between them. He'd been accused of a lot of things over the years, but being a charming social companion wasn't one of them.

Deciding he would contemplate the complexities of the female mind when he had enough time to figure it out—say, fifty years, for example—Jeremy directed Robbie's attention to the southern sky. "That's Sagittarius over there. Can you name the stars that make it up?"

"Sagittarius?" Abby asked. "That's Robbie's horoscope sign. He was born in December."

It occurred to Jeremy that by the time Robbie's sixth birthday rolled around, they'd be gone. He wondered why that knowledge didn't sit well with him.

"Every sign of the zodiac is represented in the stars," he told her. "What's your sign?"

He was just about to go into a lengthy explanation of the placement of the constellations, when Abby started to laugh. "What's so funny?" he asked.

"What's your sign? Couldn't you think of anything more original? How about 'Do you come here often?' or 'Haven't I seen you before?'"

Robbie looked back and forth between them as if trying to decipher the code they were using.

It took Jeremy a minute to get the joke, due to his limited experience with pickup lines, but he finally figured out the reason for her amusement. "I'll have you know that I would never use anything that unoriginal," he said, feigning insult.

"Really? If we had met somewhere else and you wanted to attract my attention, what would you have said?" she challenged.

The question confounded him. He had no idea what kind of conversational volley would work with someone like Abby. "How about, 'I think you're a very special woman and I'd like to get to know you better'?"

Abby's laughter faded and she looked at him levelly. "Good answer."

He had plenty of good answers, Abby thought later, as she reclined on the blanket and listened to Jeremy describe the night sky with stories of the gods and goddesses. According to him, by playing connect-the-dots with stars, you could see figures of objects or animals that were supposedly floating above. Frankly Abby couldn't see any of the heroes or beasts he pointed out but Robbie seemed to be enjoying himself.

"Tell me another one," Robbie said, attempting to hide a yawn. He'd worn himself out gazing at the sky and talking about outer space in terms Abby could barely understand. They'd finally taken a break from the telescope and had joined her on the blanket, content to lie back and stare at the stars. Abby tried not to think about the way Jeremy's body fit against hers.

"How about the story of Andromeda, the beautiful princess?'' Jeremy asked, close enough for Abby to feel his breath against her cheek.

"Was she as pretty as my mom?"

"Well, she was described as being the most breathtaking woman in all the land. So she was probably almost as pretty as your mother."

Abby snorted. If it had been anyone else piling on the flattery with that big a shovel, she'd have been suspicious about his intentions.

"What happened to her?" Robbie asked.

Jeremy told the story of the princess whose vanity got her into trouble—although Abby noticed he somehow made it sound like the real problem had stemmed from other people's jealousy. "When the hero saw her chained to a rock, he fell instantly in love," he finished the story, "flying down from the sky to rescue her from the monsters and claiming her hand in marriage."

When Robbie didn't respond with his usual follow-up question, Jeremy asked, "Not as interesting as the nine-headed monster, huh?" But looking down, he saw that Robbie had nodded off. "I think that's the first time I've actually bored someone to sleep."

Abby had noticed her son fading but she hadn't had the heart to interrupt the story. "It's past his bedtime. Sometimes I forget he's just a little boy." She turned toward Jeremy and found his face only inches from hers. "So there can be happy endings for beautiful princesses?"

"As long as the monsters don't get you first."

She thought about her ex-husband, good-looking, self-assured, smooth, and tried to picture him stargazing for Robbie's amusement. She came to one simple conclusion. Jeremy was no monster.

"I suppose we should bring him back to the car," Jeremy suggested.

"We should," she agreed.

Neither of them made any attempt to move. "Or we could wait a few minutes," she said after a while. "He looks so peaceful. Although, once he's asleep, it would take a bomb to wake him."

The silence stretched between them, thick with tension yet not uncomfortable. "You were right about tonight," he said after a while. "Canceling would have been a mistake. Thank you for encouraging me to come along."

"Encouraging?"

"Forcing, strong-arming, coercing."

"You're welcome." She smiled. "This was fun, for both of us."

"I'm glad you enjoyed it."

She'd also seen the pleasure Jeremy had gotten from watching her son soak up information he'd shared. She'd known she was right about him. He'd never be truly happy until he opened his school again.

But Jeremy's choices were none of her business. He'd made his wishes very clear. Just because she had fallen in love with him didn't give her the right to meddle in his life.

Of course, she didn't intend to let that stop her.

"If things had been different, if nothing had happened to Leonard, what do you think your life would have been like?" she asked him.

She felt him tense even though they weren't touching. "It's not worth talking about. It did happen."

"Humor me. I'm not talking about the school," she assured him. "I mean everything else. Your goals and dreams."

"How can I know what it would have been like? I can't see into the future any more than I can change the past."

"That's true." She conceded the point, knowing she

couldn't beat him in a war of words, but he had no chance against her in a battle of wills. "What would you have wanted it to be like?"

When he finally answered, she had a feeling it was more to shut her up than anything else. "The same as everyone else, I suppose. A satisfying job, a stable environment, my health."

She noticed one important item missing. "What about love?" She hadn't meant to ask the question but it slipped out.

Jeremy shifted as if he'd discovered a rock beneath him. Was she trying to destroy him? Sitting alone, in the softly scented night, it was hard enough to concentrate on the rules of this unfamiliar friendship. "You can't decide who you're going to love."

"You didn't answer the question."

He couldn't, Jeremy thought. Not even to himself. "I suppose I might have hoped to find someone I could share my life with," he admitted finally.

"Someone smart?" she asked softly.

He looked directly at her for the first time since he'd lain beside her on the softly cushioned blanket. "Yes," he responded.

Her eyes lowered.

"And strong and brave and determined and loving."

She lifted her gaze to meet his and he lost a part of himself. He couldn't imagine why it was a comforting sensation.

Unable to stop himself, he reached out to touch the strands of hair that had loosened themselves from her braid. He trailed his fingers along the thick chain of hair and tugged at the little cloth band holding it together. The strands began to part at his touch.

He rose up on one elbow to stare at her. "You really are so beautiful."

It looked as if she might want to argue the point but she didn't get the chance. Logic gone, control at an end, he leaned over and placed his mouth on hers. Her lips molded to his, soft and firm, at the same time as her eyes drifted shut.

He kept his own open, memorizing her features: the long lashes, the slope of her cheek, the translucent skin. Her beauty truly was beyond measure but her looks were only part of what made her so extraordinary. He wondered if she even knew that.

He deepened the kiss, unable to stop himself. His blood pounded in this head, clouding his thoughts. He tried to hold on to reason, knowing it was the only thing that would save him.

All his life he'd been thought of as a brain, an anomaly—a mind instead of a man. He hadn't realized before now that it had been a comfort as well as a cage.

When he was around Abby, he became human, with all of the weaknesses and desires that came along with that package. He wanted her with a ferociousness that was terrifying even to him, regardless of the fact that her son lay at her feet or that they were in the middle of a field. And if those feelings worried him, he could only imagine how they would frighten her if he let them loose.

It was only the fear of seeing that terror that allowed him some measure of control. But he couldn't restrain it completely.

Ruthlessly he ran his fingers across her skin absorbing shivers that had nothing to do with the temperature. Heartlessly he demanded more from her kiss and matched her every move. Brutally he slowed his touch until she arched wanting more.

Just as his control reached its limit, her hands began to move across his chest, his arms, his shoulders. Her touch was tentative as if she'd never touched a man before, as if she had no idea what she was doing to him. Finally he did close his eyes, experiencing sensations close to pain. Yet he didn't pull away, allowing her access to his body. When her hand dipped lower he groaned, the sound shattering the silence of the night.

She snatched her hand back as if afraid she had hurt him. She had no idea how much.

It hurt to see the way she looked at him: open, yearning, unafraid. It pained him to see the question in his eyes.

"I could—" she began, glancing across the field to his house.

"No, you couldn't," he said before she could make the offer. He wasn't sure he'd still be able to decline once he heard her say it.

She looked wounded, confused. He knew how she felt. But as much as he wanted her, he would never forgive himself if he took advantage of her temporary weakness to start something that had no place to go.

Thankfully Abby didn't push it. She took a deep breath and sat up. "Then I suppose I should get going."

He had to battle the urge not to let her leave and knew he couldn't blame his throbbing body. He wanted more than just her body, a longing that was doomed to failure. "I guess I'll see you tomorrow then," he said, forcing himself to release her. "I thought you could give me a hand organizing my office."

"The inner sanctum?" She whirled back toward him. "You're going to let me in there?"

"I don't seem to be able to keep you out." The double meaning wasn't lost on him, although she didn't seem to notice.

As a substitute to a night of hot sweaty sex, his offer seemed to do the trick. "All right. I'll see you in the morning."

"Why don't you make it the afternoon?" he suggested. "If it takes longer than expected I can make us some dinner."

She gaped at him openmouthed as if he'd just suggested she take off all her clothes and run naked through the town.

Damn. Bad analogy. His libido went into instant overdrive again, just when he'd managed to contain it. "I do know how to cook, you know."

"Oh. Of course you do. I'm sure that will be fine."

As he picked up her son and cuddled him close to his chest to keep from disturbing him, Robbie shifted in his sleep to burrow closer. Jeremy felt an unexpected well of emotion build within him. Abby turned just in time to witness it and he was helpless to do more than return the smile she gave him.

If this was friendship, Jeremy thought, he definitely wanted more.

"This place is a pigsty! How can you stand to live this way?" Abby gasped the following afternoon as she finally got a look at his office.

Jeremy squirmed visibly as she began to pick through the piles on his desk. "Those are very important articles that I have saved for a reason."

"Yeah, Mom. He's saved them for a reason," Robbie repeated, making his defection to the enemy camp clear.

Abby didn't budge, confident that the board of health was on her side. She chose one wrinkled magazine at random. "This one is older than Robbie. What could you possibly want from it now?"

"That happens to have an informative article about chaos in the universe."

"Then judging from the condition of this room, you've got it all figured out."

She saw the wince as she dumped the magazine into the recycling bin, but showed no mercy. He'd let her into this guarded room, a sign that he'd also allowed her access to so much more. She intended to make her presence known in both places.

Jeremy leaned over to Robbie and whispered, "Don't worry. I saved a copy on the computer."

Robbie giggled, delighted to be included in the effort to outsmart his mother. She didn't know whether to be happy that they'd formed a bond between them or worried that she was on the outside. She unearthed another battered magazine from the pile. "And this one? Look at it! It looks like you've been using it to swat flies."

He snatched it out of her hands before she was able to add it to the recycling. "Not that one. I want to keep it."

"Why? Does it have proof that surrounding yourself with mounds of paper has been shown to increase intelligence?"

"It has an article in it by one of my students—ex-students," he amended. "I meant to put that away."

"Oh." She looked at the worn copy he held in his hands and knew it had been looked at often. "You keep track of the kids you taught?"

"All of them that I can."

With Leonard being the exception, she knew. He seemed to have fallen off the face of the earth. And not knowing what had happened to him ate at Jeremy. She wished she could help but until she knew for sure she wouldn't say anything.

"Is there any more information about your students that you'd like to keep?"

"Actually I thought I'd removed them all before you got here."

"You went through this place already?"

"Of course. You don't think I was going to take a chance that you'd throw away something of importance, do you?"

She folded her arms across her chest and gave him a withering glare. Surprisingly he didn't melt. "Show me where you put the important stuff."

He looked to Robbie for help, but her son shrugged, knowing it was impossible to stop her once she got started. Jeremy reluctantly led the way to a walk-in closet the size of a small room where he had arranged rows of neat files with his students' names on them. She chose one at random and found a clipping from a local newspaper profiling a young lady's recent graduation from medical school.

Abby tried to imagine the amount of time and effort it took to follow the lives of each of his former students. How much did it show he cared to keep track of them, yet never to have any contact? On impulse, she rose up and wrapped her arms around his neck, planting a kiss on his lips while he stood shocked.

It didn't take him long to thaw, however, pulling her into his arms for a brief, passionate embrace. She was breathing hard by the time he pulled back.

"You are a very good man, Jeremy Waters." She held up a hand when she was sure he would disagree. "I don't want to hear it."

She led the way out of the closet and found Robbie standing nearby. It was a good thing they hadn't gotten any further carried away, she thought with relief. She didn't want Robbie to get the wrong idea about them. Despite the recent physical intimacy that had developed between them, Jeremy hadn't given her any indication that he'd changed his mind about them. She was going to have a hard enough time dealing with that when the time came, without having to disappoint Robbie, too.

Jeremy followed her out of the closet after a few moments, but the delay wasn't long enough to erase the smoldering heat in his gaze or the tightness of his body, as if struggling to hold himself in check.

She hoped she didn't look as just-kissed or Robbie would surely figure it out. She recrossed her arms over her chest, as much to feign annoyance with Jeremy as to hide her protruding nipples.

"If you think I'm going to clean up this mess, then you are out of your mind," she told him firmly.

"But you were the one who wanted to…" His voice trailed off in confusion.

"I've changed my mind. You'll have to do it yourself."

"I'll help," Robbie offered.

Although he still looked perplexed, Jeremy gave her a veiled nod of agreement.

"Call me when you're done and I'll come in to inspect it," Abby instructed, with a stern voice that she hoped masked her desire. She left before giving him a chance to disagree, heading straight outside for some deep breaths of fresh air and the hope for some answers.

Back in his office, Jeremy looked at Robbie's expectant expression. That had not worked out the way he'd expected, he thought. It had taken him hours this morning to get the room this bad. If he'd known she was going to make him clean it, he wouldn't have put quite as much effort into it. He'd thought the point was to give her a reason to come back. Since the house gleamed and she'd refused to accept his help without repayment, he didn't know what else to do to get her to stay.

"Is your mom always this bossy?" Jeremy asked, though he already knew the answer. He just didn't know why he found it so appealing.

"Yup," Robbie agreed. "You should see her when she's really mad."

Jeremy nodded in commiseration. Some things didn't need an explanation. He looked around and sighed. "Well, I suppose we should get started. What should we do first?"

"I'm pretty good at dusting," Robbie said.

"It's a deal. Let me just clear this desk off first. Want to hold the bag?"

Robbie agreed and Jeremy began to dispose of the old magazines and notebooks without bothering to look at them. They worked together silently for a time, each lost in their own thoughts.

"Do you know how many millions of germs are exchanged during a kiss?" Robbie asked suddenly.

Jeremy dropped the pile of pens and pencils he'd been gathering. They crashed to the floor, scattering in different directions like his thoughts. "Um," was all he could manage.

He looked toward the door and judged his chances for escape. The kid was small and quick, but he had panic on his side. "Is that an academic question?" he asked hopefully.

Robbie continued to stare at him inquisitively.

"I didn't think so." That was the trouble with smart kids, he thought. You could never get anything past them.

"I understand about sex," Robbie said. "I've seen the diagrams."

Jeremy flinched. How had he gotten himself into this mess? He'd been happy—relatively happy—living by himself, with no one to report to, no one to ask him questions. Especially about sex. "I, um. Maybe you should ask your mother about that."

"I'm asking you."

Yes, he was. And Jeremy had never avoided a direct question before in his life. Of course, an argument could be made that this would be a good time to start, but his conscience wouldn't allow him to evade completely. After all, there was more to this query than simple curiosity.

"There are some things that can't be explained in books," he told Robbie. "You have to find out for yourself."

"Like you're finding out with my mom?"

Like he very much *wanted* to find out with his mom— but that wasn't information he needed to share. "Something like that."

"It's okay with me if you want to be, you know, involved."

Jeremy groaned. "Where did you...? Never mind." He wasn't sure he wanted to know. But if Robbie started sharing statistics for sperm count, Jeremy was out of there.

"I think my mother has been lonely since my father left us. I don't remember him much but I know she cried when he left. It would be nice for her to have someone around who could talk to her and keep her company. Besides me."

Jeremy was incredibly touched. "I appreciate the offer. I really do. Your mother is a terrific woman. But for now we're just friends."

Robbie seemed to contemplate that answer from all angles before responding. "Are we friends, too? You know...without the kissing."

"Sure we are." Although he hadn't had any time to consider the ramifications, Jeremy knew he meant it. No matter what happened in the future he hoped he could somehow keep in touch with both Abby and Robbie. "For as long as you want to be."

"It would be nice to have someone around who understands things like I do." Robbie held out his hand to seal the bargain, appearing so much more mature than his five short years.

Jeremy shook on it, the little hand feeling awkward in his larger one.

"Friends," Robbie nodded in agreement. "As long as you don't make my mother cry like she used to."

Chapter Eleven

Abby was beginning to think he was ashamed to be seen with her. It was an unusual sensation for someone who had once been treated as nothing more than a showpiece.

She had continued going to his house, although the reasons had become blurred. She'd given up the pretense of cleaning for him since the office episode but he'd still managed to come up with reasons for her to come back each day. Gradually, without any fanfare or grand gestures, he'd begun to work with Robbie—although she wasn't sure he'd admit to actually teaching him. They'd simply begun to talk or explore or research whatever caught their attention.

Abby would have sprouted wings and flown away before she admitted that she felt left out.

Not that they purposely snubbed her. Sometimes they would try to explain the concept of chess to her or include her in one of their games. But the matches with her were over in a few quick moves while games between the two of them were intense battles of minds and wills.

They seemed to have so much in common, while Abby had begun to wonder if Jeremy would have been more interested in her if there'd been more to her than met the eye. She knew he'd enjoyed kissing her but he hadn't given any indication that he wanted more than that. She wasn't sure if he wanted anything at all since he seemed to go to great lengths not to touch her or be left alone with her.

"Checkmate," Robbie declared with a whoop of victory.

"Good one," Jeremy conceded. "I knew you had me ten moves ago but I couldn't escape. How about a rematch tomorrow so I can get even?"

Robbie bounced in his chair. "I was going to ask if we could go to the fair tomorrow instead. Did you see the posters? There is going to be a 4-H exhibit with all kinds of animals and a contest for fruits and vegetables that look like other things."

Abby had seen the advertisements for the county fair, but she'd been hoping to steal away this weekend to visit the Braitman campus. She'd been putting it off for too long.

"I don't know," Jeremy said hesitantly. "Checking out zucchini that looks like Jay Leno? What fun is that?"

"That's not all," Robbie continued. "There will be a chance to see the animals up close and they're going to have a display of genetic hybrids. You've been telling me about heredity. What better way to see it in action?"

Robbie had obviously given the idea a lot of thought. She just wished he'd talked to her in private. Jeremy clearly didn't want a repeat of the incident at the general store.

But maybe this was exactly what he needed. The chance to get out and mingle among the people and realize he was just a normal guy like the rest of them. She was certain they'd understand once they got to know him.

"Gee, Jeremy," she said, joining in. "Hybrids and heredity. What more could you want?"

She could always go to Braitman during the week, she reasoned.

He didn't look convinced, so Abby was forced to use her secret weapon. "They'll have hot dogs."

Robbie caught on quick. "And ice cream on a stick."

"And fried dough." It seemed ever since their picnic that Jeremy had discovered a craving for ordinary, everyday junk food. The more unhealthy, the better. It was yet another connection he'd found with her son.

"All right," he agreed finally. "Fried dough?"

"With powdered sugar," she added for good measure.

When he nodded reluctantly, she breathed a sigh of relief. They were staying, at least for one more day. What was the harm in that? She'd be leaving soon enough. Jeremy hadn't yet made any suggestions that they stay longer and they were running out of time. Abby had done everything she could think of to convince him, but the rest was up to him.

Jeremy licked the butter and sugar off his fingers and tried not to calculate fat grams. But it seemed a worthy trade-off for the experience. He filed the details away in his memory knowing there wouldn't be many more like this in the future—the screams of teenagers risking life and stomach contents on the plunging thrill rides, the flash of lights and the twirl of colors, the scents of suntan lotion and grilled sausage and barnyard animals. Luckily not in the same vicinity.

And Abby and Robbie. Walking by his side through the crowded lanes, touching his arm to point out a particular booth, plunking down quarters for games whose statistical odds defied reason and presenting him with their prize—a six-inch stuffed worm carrying a teacher's apple.

He clutched it in his fist and tried not to be touched.

"Look," Abby said. "Spaceship rides. Want to go take your first trip into outer space?"

"Those are for little kids," Robbie dismissed, but he watched the rockets closely as they took off from the ground and circled the crowd.

"You are a little kid," she pointed out.

"Robbie's right," Jeremy agreed. "Let's go on the Drop of Doom instead. We can test the gravitational pull as we drop ten stories."

They all looked over to the tower in the center of the amusements where it creaked dramatically as it lifted a cage of terrified-looking passengers. Suddenly the basket seemed to break free and plunge toward the ground, stopping just short of sure death. The participants stumbled off, visibly shaken, and the next group hurried to take their place.

"I suppose I can go on the rockets if it would make you happy," Robbie decided.

"It would," Abby agreed, appearing relieved. She passed him some tickets and ushered him into line.

"That was sneaky," she said when she returned.

"What good is a genius IQ if you don't get to put it to use sometimes?"

She smiled at him with a warmth that threatened to melt his neuroconductors. For a moment he forgot that they were surrounded by a throng of moms and toddlers and that her five-year-old son was standing steps away. He gave serious consideration to the possibility of sweeping her into his arms and behind the nearest concession stand.

Thankfully she turned back toward the line before reason could disintegrate completely.

"Who is Robbie talking to?" she asked.

Jeremy located Robbie's blond curls and saw him deep in conversation with a freckle-faced redhead about his age. "I don't know."

"I remember now," Abby said after a few moments. "I saw him at camp with Robbie."

They both watched closely for any sign of conflict between the two boys, but they appeared to be friends. They reached the front of the line and were ushered into the little plastic spaceships, choosing to get into the same ride rather than go separately.

"I'm going to go take a picture of them," she said. "I'll be right back."

She worked her way through the crowd to the front and began to snap pictures of the boys with a pride and excitement she might have expected if Robbie had been making his first actual space mission. Her enthusiasm was contagious and several people smiled at her as she called out to them.

That's just the way she was, he thought. Being around her made you feel happier somehow, whether you wanted to be or not. When Abby was around, he found himself smiling for no reason and looking forward to her next interruption. He thought about her constantly through the day, whether she was bothering him or not, and found himself looking forward to the next time she started a conversation he'd rather avoid. And though it usually worked against him, he admired her tenacity and the way she loved her son, putting his needs first. She was the first person he'd ever met who made him feel complete—like nothing more than a man, a state that was obvious from his near constant arousal whenever she was nearby.

His thoughts stumbled to a halt when he realized how they sounded. He might have been describing a textbook case of...

No.

He hadn't.

He couldn't have.

It was ridiculous to consider the possibility that he might have allowed amorous feelings to develop. He wasn't capable of falling in...

He couldn't finish the self-deception. He'd never understood the concept of lying to yourself. After all, what was the point? And yet, he understood it now. He couldn't even say the word to himself.

He needed to think. The lights and colors of the fair blurred as he looked for a place where he could be alone. Then he saw her coming toward him and knew it was far too late.

"Guess who we ran into? This is Sean, a friend of Robbie's from camp," Abby introduced, "and Monica, Sean's mother."

"Robbie is so cool," Sean announced proudly. "He tied up Kevin and made him cry. He stopped picking on everybody after that."

"Sean has told me so much about your son," Monica said. "He was very upset when Robbie left the camp so suddenly. You and your husband must have been very proud of the way he stood up for himself."

"Oh, um, we're not married," Abby explained hurriedly. "This is Dr. Jeremy Waters, a...friend."

"This is the Dr. Waters I've heard so much about?" Monica asked.

Jeremy automatically braced for what came next, hoping for Robbie's sake that the mother wouldn't make a scene.

"I expected you to be ten feet tall with a computer on

your shoulders instead of a head," she said with a wide, toothy smile so similar to her son's. "It's nice to have the kids look up to someone with a brain for a change instead of a rock star or a pumped-up wrestler with a bad attitude."

The comment stunned Jeremy into speechlessness, but Abby didn't appear shocked in the least. "It is, isn't it?"

"It's so hard for the intelligent children to find role models."

"I couldn't agree more," Abby responded.

As if the two women had been friends for years, they began to chat, with Monica explaining that her family had just moved to Wharton at the beginning of the summer.

Which explained, he thought, why she hadn't heard the stories about his past.

"You know, we'd love it if Robbie could come over to play someday. Being new to the area, Sean hasn't found that many friends."

"Sure, that would be great," Abby agreed.

"How about tomorrow?"

"Can I, Mom? Can I?" Robbie and Sean jumped up and down in unanimous agreement to the idea.

"Sure, that would be fine," she agreed. "I have to do some packing anyway. We're going to be heading up to Boston this week to visit a school."

The announcement caught Jeremy completely by surprise. "You're leaving?"

Jeremy hadn't realized his tone had risen until he saw Monica's eyebrows shoot up. "Oops," she said. "I didn't mean to start anything." She ushered the boys ahead to the next ride with the look of someone who recognized a fight coming when she saw one.

"Only for the day," Abby explained. "We're going to

visit Braitman. Remember, I told you I talked to someone there.''

''I remember. I just hadn't realized you were going so soon.''

''So soon? It's August already. I should have gone long before now.''

He looked for the flaw in her reasoning and found none.

''Unless you can think of any reason we shouldn't go?'' she asked.

He couldn't think at all at the moment. ''I suppose it makes sense.''

Abby nodded. ''That's what I figured.'' She turned to watch a man on stilts making his way through the crowd. ''We should probably get going before they get too far ahead of us.''

There didn't seem to be anything more to say. As they began to follow the beacon of her son's blond curls, only one thought ran through Jeremy's mind: She was leaving and life would soon be back to normal.

He tried to convince himself that he was pleased.

Abby was startled by the unfamiliar sound of a knock on her door. She hadn't had any visitors since she'd moved into town and Robbie wasn't due back from his new friend's house until this afternoon. The only other person who might have reason to stop by had made it very clear that he preferred to avoid the town at all costs.

Unless, a niggling thought crept in, the thought of her leaving had been enough to convince Jeremy he couldn't live without her. Even knowing the slim odds of that happening, her heart began to pound as she answered the door.

''May I come in?'' Jeremy asked. He looked so uncomfortable standing there, his face set in an unreadable mask. She wanted to smooth the rough lines, to pull him into her arms and erase the haunted look that never faded from his eyes. Instead she stepped back. "Of course."

She saw him scan the little cottage that had acted as their home for the summer, taking in the drab paneling and the faded paintings on the wall that could generously be called art, as well as the display of Robbie's projects and the vase of past-dead dandelions. Abby wondered why she felt so exposed having him here after she'd invaded every inch of his house and his life. Then she realized it was the first time he had come to her.

He motioned to the suitcases she'd placed in the corner. "This seems like a lot to pack for a day trip."

"I thought I'd take advantage of the time that Robbie is gone to get some work done." She'd already put together a few things for their visit but the place had been so lonely without Robbie around that she'd begun to pack up the rest of their belongings. What was the use in putting it off? No matter what they found at Braitman it was time for them to move on. She'd given Jeremy the chance to suggest otherwise but he hadn't exactly jumped at the opportunity.

"Makes sense," he agreed without any sign of emotion.

Abby turned away to drop the neatly folded T-shirt of Robbie's into the suitcase to keep him from seeing her disappointment. When was she going to learn that things couldn't always be what you wanted them to be? No matter how hard you tried.

"So what brings you to enemy territory?" she asked.

"You're not my enemy," he assured her.

"I meant the Sunshine Lodge. Mrs. Crawley's place."

"Oh, yeah." He sounded as if he'd forgotten the existence of the woman who had caused him so much trouble in the past. "I came to talk to you. I've been giving your situation a lot of thought and I've figured out a solution."

"You have?" She held her breath, waiting for him to explain.

"Yes. I've decided it would be a wise idea for me to get involved with Robbie's education. I know it's what you've been pushing for all along."

And she thought she'd been so subtle.

She couldn't believe it. Just like that. Although she'd hoped he would reach that decision, she'd honestly had her doubts. "That's great. I think that's the best solution. For both of you."

"I agree. I've already set things up with the school."

"Still Waters?" What did he mean? What was there to set up?

"No, Braitman."

"You talked to the school?"

He frowned. "I spoke directly with the dean of the college. Everything has been arranged. Robbie will be admitted without delay."

"You spoke…" It took a moment for what Jeremy was saying to sink in. He hadn't come to ask her to stay because he'd discovered he couldn't live without her, or even because he'd decided to continue teaching Robbie. He'd come to inform her that he'd made arrangements for her to go. She would have laughed if she wasn't sure she'd start to cry. "I have an appointment with the college tomorrow. We haven't even seen it yet, never mind made a decision that it's where I want him to go."

"Naturally you'll want to visit the campus, but I'm sure you'll find it suitable."

A few moments ago, she would have agreed. But ultimately, it was *her* decision. Hers and Robbie's. Surely he would understand that once she explained it to him.

"I've also arranged to be kept informed of Robbie's

progress so that I can be assured that he's getting the correct education."

"They agreed to give you that information without my permission?"

"I assured them that you would be agreeable. I knew you'd appreciate the help."

She absorbed the comment like a blow, recalling how many times her ex-husband had taken over the decision making for her own good. He, too, had been confident in his belief that she couldn't handle it alone.

"I suppose I haven't given you any reason to think otherwise," she admitted, thinking of the times she had come to him for advice.

"I have also given a great deal of thought to our relationship."

Well, at least he thought they had one. She hadn't been sure.

"I'd like to continue to see you."

Her heart jolted in her chest so strongly that she was surprised he couldn't see it. But he wasn't looking directly at her. He seemed more focused on his own thoughts, staring into space as he sometimes did when he was concentrating deeply on some complex problem.

"That sounds good to me," she answered, though he didn't seem to expect a response.

"I want you. Physically."

She found herself smiling for the first time since he'd entered the room. She couldn't even blame him for the perplexed sound of his voice. It had also taken her by surprise. "I want you, too."

"There has never been an adequate scientific explanation for sexual attraction. Some believe it's a reaction to pheromones while others suggest evolutionary causes."

As propositions went, that one needed work, she thought. But they'd have time.

"It's just chemistry," he continued. "We shouldn't allow those feelings to cloud reason."

Gradually what he was saying began to sink in. That's all it was for him? Chemistry? She'd already proved she wasn't very good at the subject. "And what have you decided would be a reasonable expectation for this... relationship?" she asked almost fearfully.

"I thought I might be able to convince you to come back to Wharton next summer. And maybe during school breaks. And perhaps I'll be able to take a trip to Boston occasionally to make sure you are both doing all right."

She didn't respond, unable to form the words that would explain how she felt by his offer.

"I don't want to rush you into anything," he continued. "We could take our time, see if you still feel it would be appropriate for us to start a discreet relationship after you've had some time to think it through."

"How thoughtful of you." She wondered what he'd say if she told him that she ached for him even now. They were alone. There was a bed in the next room. What would be his reaction if she began to take off her clothes? Would he suggest they discuss the matter or tell her she hadn't thought it through?

"During that time, if you find someone better suited to the kind of relationship you deserve then I will simply retreat with no hard feelings."

He'd retreat. With no hard feelings. "You obviously have it all figured out."

"I have tried to consider every eventuality."

And she knew, without a doubt, that it hadn't been an easy decision for him to make. He was used to being by himself, to needing no one but himself. Yet he'd been willing to make the offer of continuing a relationship between them when he could have simply let her go. She was certain it had been a huge leap for him. .

"I appreciate the offer, but I'm afraid I must decline."

"Decline? But I thought—"

She could almost feel bad for him, standing in front of her, looking at her as if she was a science experiment that had gone wrong. Almost.

"I'm afraid your offer isn't good enough. I'm not going to let you coast in and out of Robbie's life when it's convenient for you. He's already had one person who disappointed him, who didn't care enough to be there for him when it counted."

"I care about Robbie." For the first time, she heard real emotion in his voice.

"I know you do." If she was being honest with herself, she knew that he would never do anything to purposely hurt her son. In fact, he probably thought he was protecting him. She could have told him it wouldn't work. There was no way to keep yourself safe if you put your heart on the line. "You're a good man, Jeremy. I wish you would believe that. I'm sorry about what happened to Leonard. It wasn't your fault."

She didn't give him a chance to contradict her before she continued. "But everything that happened since then *is* your fault. The town doesn't hold you responsible, they're just taking their cue from you. It's not that they're afraid of you, but they don't know you. You haven't let them close enough to give them a chance."

"You don't know what you're talking about."

"Unfortunately I do. That's the problem." Because he'd done the same thing to her. "What you're offering isn't enough. Not for Robbie and not for me."

"He's a bright kid. He'll understand. It's not like he'll expect us to get married."

That one went deep. Right through her heart. "Then maybe he can explain it to me. Because I'm in love with you."

He took a step backward. "No, you're not."

His response would have been comical if it hadn't hurt so much. "I'm not?" she asked.

"You only think you're in love. It's easy to confuse infatuation, attraction, affection. This is a complicated situation. You're not thinking clearly."

Abby sucked in a painful breath. Despite everything they'd been through she hadn't realized he was capable of such cruelty.

At least he was giving her credit for having thoughts at all. She supposed she should be flattered. It had always struck her as funny that in her entire life, the only person who'd treated her as if she had a brain had been the one man who had reason to doubt it. She should have known it was too good to be true. She could never measure up. She never had.

"You're right," she confessed, concentrating on getting the words out. "I'm not thinking at all. I'm feeling. And I'm not willing to settle for less."

She shouldn't blame him. Not really. She'd barged into his life, wheedling her way into making him help her, forcing him to get involved when he'd chosen not to. For Robbie's sake and her own, she'd refused to let anything stand in her way.

But it was over. She gave up. There was nothing she could do to make him love her.

Although it was the hardest thing she'd ever done, she walked to the door and opened it. "Give me a call if you ever decide your heart is more important than your head."

Chapter Twelve

The house was quiet once again. No off-key songs, no annoying questions.

The irritation of his own company finally drove Jeremy out of the house and into the garden, where he hacked at the weeds that had begun to take root. He severed them more easily than he'd been able to cut off thoughts of Abby and Robbie.

He'd made the right decision to let her go. There could be no doubt. He wasn't used to questioning his own conclusions but this one didn't seem to leave room for error. He'd tried to give her what he thought she wanted, a relationship, an involvement, a way to keep her from walking out of his life for good.

But not love, a little voice insisted.

How could he offer her that? Even if he did have feelings for her, what kind of life would she have if she stayed? What would she have risked to be with him?

She'd been willing to risk everything, it seemed, if he were to believe her declaration of love. She'd been willing to put her heart on the line and gamble everything on her belief in him.

He'd always known she was fearless.

But that didn't mean she should have to face the mess he'd made of his life as punishment. Trying not to feel like he was the one who would be forever damned, he swung the hoe high and brought it down with an angry whack. The shock, as it connected with a stone, vibrated through his entire body.

After he stopped shaking, he bent to pick up the rock and threw it toward the house. It missed his window by inches before bouncing off the side and landing in a heap.

Jeremy caught a flash of color on the ground and walked over to investigate. There, among the high grass and the rock strewn dirt, a flower grew. Jeremy recognized the variety. The fragile yellow-white blossoms, the color of Abby's hair, were lush and exquisite. The hybrid was a cross between two different exotic flowers he'd tried to combine but that had not thrived in his greenhouse. Yet there it was, surviving in the unfriendly environment where it had been discarded.

How could it have overcome the obstacles against it? What had allowed it to flourish? Pure stubbornness, was his guess.

He thought of Abby, ignoring the barriers put in her way, going forward with what she thought was best, expecting everything and accepting nothing less.

And he thought of himself, starting with so much, being given even more, and throwing it all away. He'd made a lot of mistakes in his life, but none that felt so self-inflicted or so stupid.

Maybe, he decided, it was time for him to get smart.

Abby went on with her life. She had no choice. In a haze, she made the trip to Boston, touring the campus of what would most likely be their new home for the next few years.

If there happened to be a chunk missing out of her heart, she tried to tell herself it wasn't fatal. It was amazing, really, how much pain a person could survive and still keep going. Maybe Jeremy should do a study on it.

After a long day of travel, she pulled up in front of the Sunshine Lodge. They still had a few days left of their vacation and there had been no pressing need to stay at the new school. Besides, she still had a few things to do before they had to leave for good.

"We're home," she told Robbie.

"This is not our home," he grumbled, uncharacteristically cranky. "This is simply a place where we have lived for the last five weeks."

As usual, he was right. The lodge had never felt like home, unlike the creepy mansion where they had come to feel as if they belonged. But there was no use dwelling on something you couldn't change, she thought, dragging herself out of the car to get their bags.

Halfway up the stairs to their bungalow she stopped. A beautiful flowering plant waited for her in front of her door, the bright green ribbon tied around the base revealing it as a gift rather than something their landlord might have put there. Not that Mrs. Crawley was given to extravagant gestures.

She'd never seen anything like it before, the blossoms bold yet fragile and the most beautiful thing she had ever seen. There could be no doubt that it had come from Jeremy, but why? A token of his logical admiration? A going-away present? His reasons didn't matter. If she had any sense, she'd toss it in the trash right now and forget about it and its owner. Instead she picked it up and inhaled the sweet aroma, finally noticing the card attached.

I need to see you. Please come to my house today at four o'clock. Bring Robbie. It's important. It was signed with a scrawled J.

Abby crumpled the note in her hand. It was late—already past five since Robbie's bad mood had forced her to stop more than she'd intended on the way home. She was tired. She wanted nothing more than to go into the house and collapse on the bed, leaving the rest of her problems for another day. Whatever Jeremy wanted, it hadn't been important enough for him to stick around. And frankly, she was getting a little sick of letting him call the shots.

She should tell him that. And a few other things she'd forgotten the first time around. The image revived her flagging strength and she decided that if he wanted to see her, then she would oblige. But first, she thought maliciously, she'd take a few minutes to tidy herself up after the trip. After all, it wouldn't hurt to put her best face forward.

Out of practice in the art of cosmetics, it took her more than a half hour to get ready, but Abby thought the results were worth it. Her highlighted eyes hid any trace of puffiness, her lips, lined and glossed, looked just-kissed rather than rejected. The high heels she wore pinched her feet, but they complimented the frilly sundress that hugged her body to perfection.

She walked out of the house, ready for battle.

Her appearance didn't seem to impress Robbie, however. His complaints kept getting louder and more grating all the way to Jeremy's house.

"Now you listen to me, young man," she said as they pulled into the driveway. "I don't care if you're the smartest person in the whole world, you will not talk to me in that tone of—"

Her scolding came to a sudden halt as she saw other cars parked along the path. Lots of cars, some nearly blocking the narrow road. Something must be wrong, she thought in sudden panic. Had there been an accident? She didn't hear any sirens or see any smoke. Had the town gathered to turn against Jeremy? They'd never understood him. Maybe they'd decided to chase him out of Wharton for good.

If so, they'd have to get through her first, she thought ferociously. No matter what had happened between them, he was a good man. If anything happened to him...

She couldn't finish the thought. Racing past the rows of cars, she made her way to the house, cursing the impracticality of her heels as she charged up the stairs in front of Robbie.

She heard the noise as she reached the front door. The clatter of raised voices, the crash of breaking glass. She threw open the door, ready to come to Jeremy's rescue.

But instead, she found herself stepping into the middle of what appeared to be a party. People were packed into the small living room, standing in groups or helping themselves to trays of appetizers set up in the corner. One gentleman who appeared to have had too much to drink was picking up a broken glass and spilled liquid from the floor she'd spent hours polishing.

Abby saw several people she recognized, the pharmacist, a lady from the general store, as well as others she didn't know. A group of young men in the corner who appeared to be involved in some kind of intellectual debate stumbled into silence as, one by one, they turned to gape at her.

"Look, Mom. Sean's here," Robbie said, catching sight of his new friend. Along with Sean's mother Monica, who crossed the room to greet them.

"Whoa," Monica said, checking out her appearance with open envy. "He must have done something really stupid. Poor guy. He doesn't stand a chance."

If Abby wasn't still suffering from shock and confusion, she'd have hugged her new friend. "What's going on here?" she asked, looking around. If this was a mob, it was the friendliest one she'd ever seen.

Monica shrugged. "I got an invitation to come here this afternoon for an open house. We all did. From what I can gather, Dr. Waters spent the day yesterday hand-delivering them to anyone he could find. I think curiosity brought everyone within a ten-mile radius."

"You're kidding." Jeremy had invited all these people into his guarded ivory tower? Maybe it was worse than she'd thought. Maybe he'd suffered some kind of mental breakdown.

Just then, he rounded the corner and saw her, coming to a sudden stop in a comical faltering sort of way. He just stood there, staring at her, his gaze sweeping over her as if memorizing the details. It took every bit of Abby's strength not to move. She wanted to go to him, but she'd already put her heart on the line and had it returned to her. Whatever Jeremy had in mind, the next step had to be his.

Finally he seemed to come to his senses and he began to move toward her. It seemed to take forever for him to cross the crowded room.

"If you'll excuse me," Monica said cheerfully, "I have the sudden need to go check my face."

Rather than accompanying his friend, Robbie stepped closer to his mother. Abby glanced down in time to see a fierce protectiveness on his face that she knew would have covered her own if anyone had threatened Robbie. It broke her already shattered heart. She hadn't wanted this to happen. He'd been hurt enough. No matter how much she wanted things to be different, she had to be strong for Robbie's sake. Reaching down, she took his hand and they stood as one.

"You came," Jeremy said when he reached her. "I wasn't sure you would."

"I got your note." With an effort, she kept her voice light and breezy, like the dress that was rustling in the breeze.

He didn't answer, still staring at her in astonishment. "You look…" Words seemed to fail him. "Nice."

"Thank you." He didn't look so bad himself. A little harried, maybe, but comfortable, confident, despite the fact that a roomful of people he felt he had nothing in common with were straining their necks in an attempt to catch every word.

Abby was still reeling over the fact that while she'd been brooding over their break, he'd decided to throw a party. Obviously they were reacting to the separation differently. "What's going on here?"

Now that he had the chance to explain, he seemed to be at a loss for words. "I've been giving a lot of thought to what you said. And you were right. About the town. About a lot of things."

Her eyebrows rose. He didn't have to sound so surprised. "It happens occasionally."

He grinned as if she'd made a private joke and Abby decided there was a benefit to battle paint, after all. At least no one—especially Jeremy—would be able to see her heart breaking.

"I decided it was time to stop hiding." He looked around, still apparently in shock at the number of people who had showed up. "I invited everyone from town as well as some of my old students." The group of young men in the corner waved, not bothering to hide the fact that they were eavesdropping.

That explained some of the odd groupings she'd seen. If the situation had been different, she'd have loved to talk to some of his students in person, but finding out about Jeremy Waters was no longer in her job description.

"I think some were just curious to get a closer look at me," he whispered, leaning closer. "I'm sure the rest didn't want to miss the chance for future gossip. In any case, they came."

One of those who'd shunned him in the past came forward now. Drew Danforth's jaw dropped as he looked at her. "Abby? Oh, my God!"

Jeremy's expression changed in a flash to barely restrained violence and Drew backed away respectfully. "I, um, I owe you an apology. And Robbie." He looked down at her son, who hadn't budged from her side. "I should have been in better control of the situation at camp. I'm afraid I wasn't thinking too clearly. Frankly I was trying to impress you. I guess it backfired."

"There was no harm done," Abby said, recalling that the incident had allowed Robbie to get close to Jeremy. The harm had come afterward.

"What about you, buddy?" Drew ruffled Robbie's curls. Her son rolled his eyes in response. "Do you forgive me, too?"

"I guess so," Robbie answered.

"I suppose we all make mistakes. Even Waters, here. He finally clued us in to what's been going on. I have to tell you, all this secrecy made people pretty curious."

"I've talked to some people about exactly what happened before, including my part in it," Jeremy clarified. "It seems it was my evasiveness rather than the incident itself that they resented. I promised to be more forthcoming in the future.''

''That's good,'' she said, her happiness for him almost bringing tears to her eyes despite everything. Now he'd have a chance for a normal life. She'd always known the town would open up once he gave them the opportunity. If only he'd realized it sooner.

When Drew realized neither of them seemed to remember he was still there, he gave up and wandered away.

''I've even given some thought to opening the school again,'' Jeremy told her. ''Not like it was before but maybe in conjunction with the high school, as an enrichment program for children of all ages and learning abilities. That way the kids I taught wouldn't feel so different.''

''That sounds great,'' she said, meaning it. It would be the perfect solution.

He swallowed, appearing nervous and unsure of himself for the first time since she'd met him. ''Would you and Robbie consider coming back?''

Her mouth dropped as she heard the offer. He'd asked her to return to Wharton, to be a part of his life. They could make it work, after all. It wouldn't be all that she'd wanted, but maybe it could be enough. She looked down at Robbie and thought of all she'd been through to make sure he got what he deserved. She knew Jeremy would be a great teacher. Robbie couldn't have asked for more.

But she could.

She wouldn't put herself through that again, feeling less than adequate, never measuring up. For once, she refused to settle for less than everything she deserved—a man who respected her. A man who loved her. A man who couldn't live without her.

Apparently Jeremy Waters was not that man.

''I'm sorry, but that's not good enough.''

The crowd gasped. Abby would have given anything not to have played this out in front of everyone, but she didn't seem to have a choice. "Maybe we should talk about this in private."

"I'm done hiding," he responded, appearing frankly dumbfounded by her answer. "I thought...I thought now that I'd settled all this, there'd be nothing stopping us. You can come back. It can be just like it was."

"I don't want it like it was," she said, wincing in pain that was nearly unbearable. He was giving her a chance to stay, to give Robbie a life where he would fit in.

But Abby deserved more. He'd been the one to teach her that.

Jeremy didn't know what to say. She wouldn't come back. It was too late. There was nothing he could do to convince her that he'd changed, that he needed her with a ferocity he could no longer fight.

He wasn't going to give up, he decided. She'd taught him that much at least. But he didn't know what else to do. Because of his mistakes, she would leave for good and take Robbie. They would go to a place where the teachers weren't wounded and where the men weren't cowards. He might never see them again. Although he'd given a great deal of thought to Abby's role in his life, he hadn't realized how much he would miss the boy.

He knelt in front of Robbie and saw the distrust and hurt he didn't bother to hide. "I guess I let you down, after all. I'm so sorry. Will you forgive me, too?" Jeremy asked.

This time the pardon wasn't so easily given. Robbie stared at him unflinchingly. "You made my mother cry."

Jeremy couldn't blame him for his protectiveness. He'd have battled anyone who had treated her like he had. "I did. And I'm sorry. I'll try never to do it again, but I might mess up sometimes. When two people love each other, they can hurt each other without meaning to."

"What did you say?" Abby blurted.

"I was just explaining that sometimes fights don't mean—"

"Not about that! About loving me."

"Well, of course I do. Why else would I have gone through all this?"

"Oh, man," someone in the crowd groaned. "I thought you said he was a genius? He's just a regular dope like the rest of us."

"Why didn't you say so?" Abby asked.

"I didn't think I— I didn't think," he amended. "I'm afraid I'm not very good at this. I've never fallen in love before."

He stood up and started to ruffle Robbie's curls before thinking better of it and taking his hand instead. When he lifted Abby's other hand and held it in his, the three of them made a circle. "I'm just a man," his voice was soft, pleading. "I made a mistake."

"You?"

"I'm afraid so. I let you go. How stupid can a person get?"

"That's pretty dumb," she agreed. Her smile transformed her face to something more beautiful than perfection. There were tears in her eyes but for once he wasn't ashamed to have put them there.

"I love you," he said finally, "madly, completely, foolishly. You make me whole. Come back and let me prove it to you."

"Are you sure?"

"I've never been as sure about anything."

"Considering how much you know, I guess that's a lot."

"It's more than enough," he promised. "I love you. Let me spend the next fifty years showing you."

"Only fifty?"

"Well, considering the median age— Let's just see what happens."

It was apparently the right thing to say. "You know me pretty well."

"Not as well as I want to." He made her a silent vow of countless hours of exploration. "Come back," he pleaded. "You can teach me."

As she nodded, the crowd cheered and they rushed together, with Robbie whisked up in his arms to join in the embrace.

He still had a lot to learn, Jeremy thought, but it was a lesson he was looking forward to.

* * * * *

**Where royalty and romance
go hand in hand...**

The series continues in Silhouette Romance
with these unforgettable novels:

HER ROYAL HUSBAND
by Cara Colter
on sale July 2002 (SR #1600)

THE PRINCESS HAS AMNESIA!
by Patricia Thayer
on sale August 2002 (SR #1606)

SEARCHING FOR HER PRINCE
by Karen Rose Smith
on sale September 2002 (SR #1612)

And look for more Crown and Glory stories in
SILHOUETTE DESIRE starting in October 2002!

Available at your favorite retail outlet.

Where love comes alive™

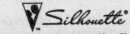

SILHOUETTE *Romance*

COMING NEXT MONTH